THE DEAD CAN'T SPEAK

DI SARA RAMSEY #3

M A COMLEY

JEAMEL PUBLISHING LIMITED

COPYRIGHT

ACKNOWLEDGEMENTS

Thank you as always to my rock, Jean, I'd be lost without you in my life.

Special thanks to Studioenp for creating such a superb cover.

My heartfelt thanks go to my wonderful editor Emmy Ellis @ Studioenp and to my fabulous proofreaders Joseph, Jacqueline, and Barbara for spotting all the lingering nits.

And finally, thank you to all the members of my wonderful ARC group for coming on this special journey with me and helping me to grow as an author. Love you all.

ALSO BY M A COMLEY

Blind Justice (Novella)
Cruel Justice (Book #1)
Mortal Justice (Novella)
Impeding Justice (Book #2)
Final Justice (Book #3)
Foul Justice (Book #4)
Guaranteed Justice (Book #5)
Ultimate Justice (Book #6)
Virtual Justice (Book #7)
Hostile Justice (Book #8)
Tortured Justice (Book #9)
Rough Justice (Book #10)
Dubious Justice (Book #11)
Calculated Justice (Book #12)
Twisted Justice (Book #13)
Justice at Christmas (Short Story)
Prime Justice (Book #14)
Heroic Justice (Book #15)
Shameful Justice (Book #16)
Immoral Justice (Book #17)

Toxic Justice (Book #18)
Unfair Justice (a 10,000 word short story)
Irrational Justice (a 10,000 word short story)
Seeking Justice (a 15,000 word novella)

Clever Deception (co-written by Linda S Prather)
Tragic Deception (co-written by Linda S Prather)
Sinful Deception (co-written by Linda S Prather)
No Right To Kill (DI Sara Ramsey Book 1)
Killer Blow (DI Sara Ramsey Book 2)
The Dead Can't Speak (DI Sara Ramsey Book 3)
Deluded (DI Sara Ramsey Book 4) Due out May 2019

Forever Watching You (DI Miranda Carr thriller)
Wrong Place (DI Sally Parker thriller #1)
No Hiding Place (DI Sally Parker thriller #2) Cold Case (DI Sally
Parker thriller#3)
Deadly Encounter (DI Sally Parker thriller #4)
Lost Innocence (DI Sally Parker thriller #5)
Web of Deceit (DI Sally Parker Novella with Tara Lyons)
The Missing Children (DI Kayli Bright #1)
Killer On The Run (DI Kayli Bright #2)
Hidden Agenda (DI Kayli Bright #3)

Murderous Betrayal (Kayli Bright #4)
Dying Breath (Kayli Bright #5)
The Hostage Takers (DI Kayli Bright Novella)
The Caller (co-written with Tara Lyons)
Evil In Disguise – a novel based on True events
Deadly Act (Hero series novella)
Torn Apart (Hero series #1)
End Result (Hero series #2)
In Plain Sight (Hero Series #3)
Double Jeopardy (Hero Series #4)
Sole Intention (Intention series #1)

Grave Intention (Intention series #2)
Devious Intention (Intention #3)
Merry Widow (A Lorne Simpkins short story)

It's A Dog's Life (A Lorne Simpkins short story)
A Time To Heal (A Sweet Romance)
A Time For Change (A Sweet Romance)
High Spirits
The Temptation series (Romantic Suspense/New Adult Novellas)
Past Temptation Lost Temptation

Books to come.

Tempting Christa (co-written by Tracie Delaney coming in April 2019)

Avenging Christa (co-written by Tracie Delaney coming in May 2019)

The Man In The House (co-written by Emmy Ellis coming in May 2019)

PROLOGUE

THE NIGHT WAS CHILLIER than she'd anticipated as she waited on the corner for him to meet her. Mid-March, and she was rubbing her hands together to keep warm. Mind you, if she'd bothered to put more layers on like her mother had always drilled into her as a kid, she'd probably be able to combat the cold better. *That's tough. I can't look sexy in jeans and a woolly jumper.* She stamped her feet, her four-inch heels clicking against the pavement, sending tiny jolts of pain shuddering up her slim calves. *What women have to do to please the opposite sex.*

A couple of young men passed her, whispering, leering at her as they got closer. A shudder rippled up her spine. *Do one, idiots, I'm out of your class.* She glanced up the road but kept half an eye on them in case they decided to double back and pounce on her. *Men! What gives them the right to letch like that? To ogle every girl they pass in the street? Tossers, the lot of them. All except one, that is!*

Another ten minutes dragged past. Her gaze drifted up to the clock in the main square for the seventy-fifth time in the fifteen minutes she'd been standing there, freezing her bits off. A hot breath on her neck had her yelping. She turned, and the second she laid eyes on his handsome features, she was lost. If any other man had kept her

1

waiting for two minutes, let alone fifteen, she would have been livid. Punched his lights out for having the audacity. But this man, well, he knew he had a special place in her heart. Yes, now and then he abused her—not physically, no, he'd never done that, but mentally. Was it really abuse, though? Or was it his way of tormenting her, teasing her, ensuring she was at fever pitch for him.

Whatever his reason was for being late, she'd forgive him, she always did. She was that besotted with him that she didn't care how he treated her, as long as he made the time to be with her. He was a busy man with a tight schedule. She'd known that from the outset of their relationship and had accepted it.

"There you are. I was beginning to think you'd forgotten me." She smiled and fluttered her false eyelashes.

He placed a hand on either side of her face and pulled her closer, his lips light as he tenderly kissed her. "It would be impossible to forget about you. Sex on legs and a beauty men would kill for."

His seductive tone ensured she melted into his arms, and they shared a long, satisfying kiss that stirred her insides, whisking them into a frenzy. She wanted this man so much, sometimes the pain was unbearable, so real it physically hurt.

"Do you want to eat? Or shall we go straight back to your hotel? I know which I'd prefer," he asked.

Under the glare of the streetlights, she picked up on the added glint in his eye and soon forgot the hunger pains she'd suffered for the past fifteen minutes while waiting for him to show up. "My hotel, or yours? Remind me why we're staying in different hotels again?"

"Out of necessity. I have several business meetings planned over the coming few days. If we stayed in the same hotel, the temptation of having you close would have a detrimental effect on me. You know how much I *adore* you, princess."

He'd used her special name. Her cheeks warmed, and a shyness overwhelmed her. "I'm so lucky to have you in my life."

"No, I'm the lucky one. What man wouldn't be wildly happy to have a beautiful girl like you on his arm? Shall we go?"

Her insides tingled, and she blocked out the shivers against the cold that had consumed her. She hooked her arm through his, her excitement mounting. Together they walked the three hundred yards to her hotel. She went towards the lift, but he pulled her back.

"I fancy going up the stairs instead," he said.

She never questioned what he wanted, was always happy to go along with his suggestions, inside and outside the bedroom. He was a man of the world, knew his own mind and what he wanted out of life, and she was more than content to comply with his wishes.

She placed her card in the door, and it sprang open. She glanced over at the bed. It was tidy. She let out a relieved sigh, suddenly remembering that she'd tidied it herself before she'd left the room, in the hope that he would suggest coming back here.

He slipped her thin jacket from her shoulders and stood back to admire the slinky, above-the-knee dress she had chosen. "Stunning. You're almost good enough to eat."

She quivered under his seductive gaze. He stepped forward and took her in his arms. They fitted together like chocolate and champagne. She eased off one shoe and dropped four inches.

He shook his head. "Keep them on. I love seeing you naked in heels."

His hands worked with a gentleness she'd come to expect from him as he undressed her. Snuggling into her neck, inhaling her Poison perfume, he sighed and brushed his lips against her skin. It tickled when he told her how much he wanted her.

Naked, except for her sexy black hold-ups and heels, he tipped her back on the bed and stared at her, taking in every inch of her slender body and accentuating curves. Her gaze dropped to the bulge in his trousers, and her heart skipped several beats, the excitement elevating her even higher. Desperate to have him, she held out her hand, inviting him onto the bed, not caring if he was fully clothed or not. She needed him beside her, now.

He took her hand and inched his way towards her. Her breath caught in her throat; the anticipation was killing her. He was a master teaser, knowing that it amplified the experience.

After kissing the length of her body and moaning with desire, he flipped her over and pulled her up on her knees. His hands covered her breasts then began their journey downwards. She was desperate to rid him of his clothes; however, she remained silent, knowing how much he preferred to take charge of their sexual encounters.

And boy was he in control. The more he touched her, the more her senses were heightened and the more she wanted him. He was an expert lover. She'd never known such depths of desire in her life until she'd met him. She was lost, allowing him to explore her, moaning her satisfaction as his hands touched every inch of her tingling skin.

"How is it, baby?"

"Good, so good. But I want to see you, feel your skin next to mine," she said, her voice strained with an overwhelming lust.

"Ssh...patience. You'll feel me soon enough," he whispered, his words seductive against her ear.

His hands traced a sensuous line over her throat. She fell under his spell once more. She loved it when he touched her there.

"How's that? You want more? Want to try something different tonight?"

Her tongue, swollen with desire, just like every other part of her body, restricted her ability to answer him. Instead, she nodded enthusiastically.

His hands continued to glide across the taut skin of her throat, massaging her tenderly until his fingers tightened around her windpipe. She moaned. His fingers squeezed even tighter.

Panic set in. "Please, stop, you're hurting me."

His tongue lashed her cheek. "Ssh...enjoy the moment. Relax, it'll all be over soon enough."

She tried her utmost to relax, but his grip tightened as the breath continued to seep out of her body. She flailed her arms. "Please...no more. Stop."

"Why? You love it when I show you attention like this. Love it. Relax. Go with the flow."

"Not like this. You're hurting me," she croaked out her reply.

Unexpectedly his tone switched, his words taking on a more sinister note, pushing aside his persuasive whisper. "You think you're so damn sexy, don't you? Think you cast a spell over the men you lure into your bed? Not this man. You *disgust* me, slut. You always have done. I used you. I've never loved you, even though I might have said the words. I could never love a desperate slut like you. A woman willing to spread her legs at the flick of a switch. Look at you now, me fully clothed and you stark naked. Whore! You're nothing but a revolting whore."

The words stung, but her thoughts remained on her efforts of trying to unlatch his fingers from her throat. The more she fought, the more he rebelled and spoke filth in her ear.

"How naïve of you to think I'd ever be interested in a piece of shit like you. You had your uses. I screwed you when the urge to fuck someone grew too much. I hated every damn minute of it. Shudder at the thought of my cock between your legs. You repulse me."

She choked, hot tears streaming down her inflamed cheeks. It was then that it registered with her what his intention was. She bucked, tried to dislodge his hands, but his hold became firmer, her windpipe squeezing tightly shut, the air being sucked out of her.

"Please…" she pleaded in nothing more than a pitiful whisper. "I'll do anything you ask."

He laughed, tilting his head back away from hers. She struggled to keep upright. The breath escaped her body quickly now, all fight in her fading fast. Her life, the wonderful life she had led before she'd met this man, a generation away from her now. She was desperate to see the mother she loved, the sister she'd always fought with during their teenage years. Their faces filled her mind as her last breath faded.

His hands hurt. One final squeeze, and the deed should be complete. Her body went limp beneath his touch; however, he intensified his grip, just in case she was faking it—some of the others had resorted to that to try to fool him. Satisfied she was now dead, he pushed her away and withdrew a handkerchief from his pocket, wiping the feel of her disgusting skin from his hands. He thought about visiting the bathroom but didn't want to leave any of his DNA in there for the cops to find.

Next, he slipped on a pair of gloves and searched the room, looking for her ID. He found it in her handbag. In her purse he located a debit card. He hunted the pockets of her bag and stumbled across a slip of paper with her PIN written on it. He rubbed his hands together, knowing she'd recently been paid a bonus at work. He'd steal that money, or how much the hole in the wall allowed him to have in one hit, and be on his merry way before her body was discovered. He took every form of ID lying in her bag. An idea formed in his head, and he chuckled. He'd make it super difficult for the police to find him.

For now, he needed to get out of there. He opened the door and peered around the doorframe. The corridor was empty. He left the room and quietly closed the door behind him, making sure he didn't attract the attention of any possible nosy parkers on either side.

He left via the stairs and kept his head down as he passed the reception desk. Thankfully, the receptionist was dealing with a guest, and he exhaled the breath that was burning his lungs.

Once outside, he ventured up the high street to the nearest cash machine. His hat tilted to cover his face from the camera, he inserted the PIN he'd memorised and withdrew the maximum allowed, three hundred pounds, which he inserted in his wallet. He jauntily strolled down the rest of the street, safe in the knowledge that his disguise would distort any likely CCTV images, and around the corner to the hotel where he was staying, whistling a merry tune as if he didn't have a care in the world. He had plenty, but he was dealing with them.

Ticking names off a list, one by one...

CHAPTER 1

DI Sara Ramsey stroked her cat, Misty, and left the house. Out of habit, she checked the immediate vicinity. Once she was confident it was safe to proceed, she dashed along the path to her car, cursing that she hadn't emptied the garage yet. She needed to get around to doing that this weekend if her safety was being threatened.

After numerous incidents of vandalism had blighted her life, she had received a call from DI James Smart back in Liverpool, informing her he had arrested Wade, the gang leader involved in her husband's death. While she'd been elated to hear such news, he was quick to add a warning during their conversation. A warning that had unnerved her ever since: the gang members were about to target her, their aim to intimidate her into possibly influencing the outcome of their leader's fate in the courtroom. How the heck she was supposed to do that, she didn't have a clue. She was scared, not for her own safety, but for that of her loved ones.

The second Smart had told her everything, what had happened recently on the vandalism front started to make sense. The bastards had even poured paint stripper over her boyfriend's car. They had also daubed a vicious slogan in red paint on her door, thrown a stone with a threatening message through her window and previously poisoned her beloved cat. As a vet, Mark, her boyfriend, had been the one who had thankfully saved Misty's life.

Now, since having that conversation with Smart, her days were spent vigilantly looking over her shoulder, ensuring no one unexpectedly pounced on her. How long she'd put up with feeling so fraught and inept, she had no idea. As it was, her sleep had suffered in the last few weeks, as had her relationship with Mark. She was determined to keep him at arm's length, for his own safety. She'd already lost one love of her life to this vile gang, she wasn't about to lose another. Was that how she felt about him? Did she love him? They'd only been seeing each other a few months. He'd treated her well so far. Hadn't forced himself upon her like other men would have. He'd understood she was still grieving for Philip, even after two years of her husband dying in her arms.

The journey into work was conducted through the usual fear debilitating her life at present. She hated being in this state, in limbo, not knowing when or if a possible strike was about to happen. She ground her teeth as she parked in her allocated space at the station and got out of the car.

The welcome smile of Jeff, the desk sergeant, greeted her the second she stepped through the main entrance.

"Good morning, ma'am. Another bright spring day ahead of us."

"Bit nippy during the night, Jeff. At least the sun is out today, though, something to be grateful for, I suppose. Anything new come in overnight?"

The smile dropped. "I've just left a note on your desk, ma'am. A murder in a hotel room in town, at the Red Dragon Hotel. Not pleasant."

Sara rolled her eyes. "Is any murder pleasant? Have the rest of my team arrived yet, do you know?"

"All bar one, I believe."

"Good. Carla and I will get over to the hotel ASAP."

"Ah, she's the bar one."

Sara furrowed her brow. "Really? Wow, you have surprised me.

She's usually the first in most days. I'd better give her a ring, see if everything is all right."

Just then the entrance door opened, and a dishevelled-looking Carla marched in. "Morning. Cripes, not late, am I? Why are my ears burning?"

"No. I've only just arrived myself. Is everything all right?"

Carla rushed past her. "Yes, why shouldn't it be?"

Sara cringed, pulled a face at Jeff and hurried after Carla. "Hey, stop."

Carla halted on the stairs ahead of her but didn't turn around.

Sara caught up and peered at her face. "What's wrong?"

"Nothing," Carla replied sharply.

"Of course there's not. How silly of me to think such a thing. Don't frigging kid a kidder, love. In the ladies' toilet, pronto." Sara ran on ahead and positioned herself by the sink, her arms folded, tapping her foot as she waited for her partner to join her.

Carla entered the toilet with her head down.

"Hey, what's wrong?"

Carla walked into the cubicle, tore off a few sheets of toilet paper and blew her nose. She returned and stood in front of Sara. "Nothing more than usual. I'm sorry I'm not beaming from ear to ear. I'm kinda feeling like shit lately, since finishing with Andrew."

Sara rubbed her hand up and down her partner's arm. "Jesus, I'm sorry. I should learn to keep my mouth shut. I thought you'd be over him by now."

"It's only been a few weeks since I kicked him out. You're still not over the death of your husband, so you're hardly in a position to speak, are you?"

"Ouch! For a start, Philip was murdered. Correct me if I'm wrong here, but you caught Andrew fooling around with a trollop. It's hardly the same thing, love."

Carla slammed her back against the sink close to Sara. "Shit. Ignore me. I'm screwed, consumed with loneliness."

"Bollocks. All you need is a night out on the town with your mates.

Pick up the first man who shows an interest in you and shag him until you can't walk."

Carla stared at her, mouth gaping.

"Do you mind? That's not a pleasant view first thing in the morning. My toast and marmalade almost made a reappearance then. Stop with the self-pity. There's only going to be one winner if you persist in punishing yourself in that way, and that's scumbag Andrew. Don't let the bastard win. He's soooo not worth it."

"I know you're right. It's hard, though. How did you cope with not having a man around for two years?"

She shrugged. "Grief is a great companion. Well, that and Misty."

Carla cracked her face and smiled. "You're a nutter!"

"Guilty as charged. Right, we need to plod on; we've got a murder on our hands. Remind me why I moved to this area again? Ah yes, for a more peaceful life where crime rates were far lower than Liverpool. Guess what? That's frigging changing faster than a speeding bullet."

"At least you're not blaming yourself nowadays for the situation altering, not like you used to."

"I have to accept it's a sign of the times. That people are far angrier nowadays and keen to hand out retribution rather than have a frank discussion with each other to air their grievances. What a crappy world we live in, and here's even bigger news, it's getting crappier by the second by all accounts. Blow your konk again, you've got a bogey hanging." She hadn't, but Sara loved seeing her partner jump into action through embarrassment. She left the toilet laughing as Carla spun around to the mirror to check her appearance. "Gotcha."

Carla's laugh followed her up the corridor and into the incident room. The whole team glanced her way and either smiled or said good morning.

"Morning, all. Carla is here; she's just sorting out her bogeys in the toilet." She looked over her shoulder when the door opened mid-sentence and found a mortified Carla standing in the doorway, the colour swiftly rising into her cheeks. "I'm joking. Right, we haven't even got time for a coffee this morning. So much for easing us gently

THE DEAD CAN'T SPEAK

into our working day. I need to check my office first, but it would appear we have a murder case on our hands."

"Would that be the one at the Red Dragon Hotel, boss?" Barry Thomas asked in his subtle Welsh lilt.

"Crap, don't tell me it's been on the news already?"

Barry nodded. "Yep, heard a snippet about it on the radio on the way in this morning."

Sara preferred to hear music in the car first thing, not the news. Maybe she should reconsider that in the future. "Damn, we'd better get over there, Carla. There's bound to be a press presence at the scene." Sara nipped into her office and collected the note about the crime from her desk. She returned to the incident room to find Carla missing. "Blimey, she's keen. Okay, team, you know what to do. I want CCTV footage gathered for a start. I haven't got a name for the victim as yet, so we can't do anything else unfortunately. Barry, you and Craig deal with the cameras for me. Hopefully we'll have more information for you when we return."

Sara rushed out of the incident room and down the stairs. She found Carla standing by her car, face up to the sky, bathing in the early morning sun's rays. "Now I can understand your hurry. Come on, we haven't got time to top up our tans."

"Truth be told, I needed to escape your vicious tongue."

Sara chuckled. "Seriously? Vicious? If you think that was vicious, matey, you wait until we really fall out."

Carla's mouth gaped open again.

"Bloody hell, that's twice you've shared that view with me today. A third time, and I'll put you down for unpaid overtime."

Carla snorted. "Like you don't already. Maybe the hours I put in around here are the cause of my relationship problems."

"You really are feeling sorry for yourself today, aren't you? Buck up, love. The chance to meet a nice new fella will come your way soon enough, guaranteed."

They drove to the hotel, which was a few miles away, in relative silence. As predicted, there were hordes of reporters, some local, some from the national newspapers, standing on the steps of the hotel.

"Jesus. When are these guys going to learn to back off a bit? Where's the frigging cordon gone?"

Carla spotted the blue-and-white crime scene tape lying on the concrete steps of the hotel. "Looks like they broke through it. Want me to call for backup?"

"Do it. I'll have a quick word. Doubt if it's going to do much good, but I'll have to try."

They left the car. Carla rang the station while Sara barged through the throng of reporters and made it to the front.

"Guys, give us a break, will you? I know you're all eager for the story, but, as of this moment, I've got nothing to share with you. Not likely to have anything for a few hours. Take my advice and go find somewhere to have a fry-up and wet your whistle with a cuppa, okay?"

"It's DI Ramsey, if I'm not mistaken?" a young reporter from the local TV station asked. He thrust a microphone under her nose and glanced over his shoulder at his cameraman to check if he was filming the interview, if there was one.

She raised her hand. "It is. There's no point asking me anything. Right now, you probably know as much as I do. Let me get inside and see for myself what's going on, and I promise to get back to you shortly."

"A likely story, Inspector," the same reporter mumbled.

"It is what it is. Don't push me for answers I refuse to divulge, not because I don't want to tell you, but as I've already stated, I can't. I'm in the dark myself until I see the victim. Okay? Thanks for your patience, ladies and gents. Now, if you wouldn't mind going back beyond the cordon. You know the rules; don't make me come down heavy on you. I could always move the cordon back a mile or so if you persist in being disruptive."

There were two uniformed constables standing at the entrance to the hotel looking as if they were out of their depth.

She approached them and leant in. "Don't allow them any nearer. We've called for backup. I know this isn't your fault. Once the press pack get a whiff of a murder, they tend to up their game. We've got to do the same, gentlemen. Got that?"

"Yes, ma'am. They just swamped us. Didn't even give us a chance to erect the cordon properly. I must admit, we were overwhelmed when their mob mentality kicked in," the younger of the two constables said, fear emanating in his eyes.

"Don't apologise. I know exactly how this went down. You'll be more alert next time." She smiled and patted both men on the shoulders as Carla joined her.

"Reinforcements are on the way, chaps. That'll upset them. Watch out for the backlash," Carla warned.

Sara snorted. "They wouldn't dare. They need to keep us sweet if they want to stay in business. No one has managed to get into the hotel, have they?"

"No one, ma'am. We've been extra vigilant to ensure that didn't happen."

"Good. Hang in there. The troops should be with you soon." Sara nodded and swept past the two officers and into the entrance through the rotating doors.

The main reception area was grander than the exterior of the hotel which, according to the date stone Sara had spotted on the way in above the entrance, dated back to nineteen-twelve. Something in the back of Sara's mind told her they had recently had a refurbishment.

She and Carla approached the black-haired receptionist. She revealed crooked teeth when she smiled at them. "Hello. Sorry for the disruption outside. The police are doing their best to keep it to a minimum. Do you have a reservation with us?"

Sara flipped open her warrant card and showed it to the woman. Carla did the same. "No need to apologise, we're here on official business. DI Sara Ramsey and DS Carla Jameson. Is the manager around?"

"Manageress, yes. I'll get her for you." The receptionist walked away from the desk and disappeared around the curved corner behind her. She emerged a few seconds later with a tall, smartly dressed blonde woman in tow.

The blonde offered her hand. Sara shook it.

"DI Sara Ramsey, and you are?"

"Nigella Windsor. I'm the manageress around here—for my sins. Well, I'm glad you're here. Maybe you can address that mob out there, force them back a little so we can keep trading."

"Already actioned. We've called for backup. You're aware the hotel will be treated as a crime scene, aren't you?"

"All of it? We're fully booked. I can't start kicking the guests out."

"I'll have a word with the Scene of Crime Officers, see if we can get away with sectioning off the floor where the murder took place. If not, then your guests are going to have to make alternative arrangements, at least for a day or two."

"Goodness me. That's going to damage our reputation. Just when it's at its peak, too."

Sara hitched up a shoulder. "Sorry about that. Hopefully, we won't be too disruptive for long. Would you mind showing us to the room?"

"Of course. Come this way. We'll go up in the lift."

The ride was a smooth, rapid one. The doors *swooshed* open on the fourth floor.

"There's a camera in the lift. We'll need to have a copy of the footage for evidence—by the end of the day if possible."

"Consider it done. Here you go, room four-o-five. Will you be needing me for anything else?"

"Not at the moment. If you can arrange for us to have any footage you have from the cameras dotted around the hotel, the reception area and outside the main entrance if you have them, that would be a great help."

"I'll sort that out and have it ready for when you leave."

"Thanks," Sara said, dismissing the woman by turning her back on her and entering the room.

Pathologist Lorraine Dixon, with her bright-red hair draped around her shoulders, was already in the room, organising her team. She glanced over and nodded as they entered and returned to instructing the man in the white suit, holding the camera, of what she needed next. "Let me know when you've finished, and I'll proceed myself." She left the man and stepped forward a few paces. "Going to have to ask you to tog up, ladies. No one is allowed any farther without the correct gear on. Glad you're here for this one. Rather unpleasant in nature." She bent down and extracted two white suits and blue plastic shoes from a box close to the door and handed them to Sara and Carla, who slipped them on whilst continuing the conversation with Lorraine.

"Do we have any ID for her?" Sara nodded towards the bed at the naked victim.

"As far as I can tell, there's nothing here to indicate who she is. Maybe the hotel staff can fill in the blanks there."

"We'll check on that when we leave the room. COD?"

"Strangulation."

"I'm taking it that she had sex before she was murdered?"

"Only just got here myself so haven't got around to examining her thoroughly as yet. Let my guy take the photos, and we'll do it together, if you like?"

"I don't mind. All right if we have a nosy at her things?" Sara asked, snapping on a pair of gloves.

"Go for it. There's an overnight bag in the bottom of the wardrobe. All her belongings are either hanging up or placed in the drawers."

"She intended to or had stayed for a few days then, right?"

"That's my take on things."

Sara opened the wardrobe doors and peered at the clothes on the rail. A few business suits, and that was it. No jeans, nothing to say this was anything but a business trip. She glanced over her shoulder at the slinky red dress scrunched up on the furry white rug lying close to the bed. "All business attire except for that. She met someone. The question is, was she on the pull or did she know her assailant?"

Lorraine nodded and smiled. "I pretty much came to the same conclusion."

"I have a notion, if you want to hear it," Carla piped up.

"Feel free to chip in, partner," Sara prompted.

"Could she be a sex worker?"

Sara chewed her lip. "Ordinarily, I'd say yes. However, looking at the clothes hanging in her wardrobe, I'd have to discount that idea."

Carla shrugged. "Sorry."

Sara smiled and took a step closer to the bed to assess the body. "Any obvious signs of DNA, stray hairs or anything yet?"

Lorraine stood alongside her while her technician fired off the last of his shots and stepped aside. "Haven't seen anything obvious as yet."

Scratching the back of her head, Sara groaned. "Where the hell do we begin with this one, with no bloody ID to go on?"

"You've got your work cut out for you, that's for sure," Lorraine replied. "I'll do my best to have the results of the PM for you in a few days."

"Can I make another suggestion?" Carla asked tentatively.

Sara frowned. Twice in the space of two minutes her partner had asked that. It was totally unlike her. "Shoot."

"We're going to have to ask the media for help, right?"

Sara nodded. "Yep, looks that way. What's your point, Carla?"

"I'll have a word with reception, see if they've got a photo of her we can share with the press."

"Good idea. Actually, if there's nothing else for us here, Lorraine, I'd like to start questioning the staff, what with time being of the essence and the fact there's a murderer on the loose."

Lorraine waved. "Go. I'll be in touch soon."

"One thing before I leave. Can you give me a rough time of death to go on?"

"A guesstimate from the body temperature I took a few minutes ago would be somewhere between seven and ten p.m. at this point."

"That's great. Thanks, Lorraine. We'll leave you to it."

Lorraine placed her bag on the bed beside the victim and opened it.

Carla appeared fascinated by the instruments the pathologist was withdrawing from her bag.

Sara pulled her arm. "Come on, you, we have work to do."

They stripped off their suits and placed them in a black bag near the door and left the room.

In the hallway, Sara turned to face Carla. "Are you all right?"

"Yes, why?"

"You asked two questions in there—correction, you volunteered two notions in there, in an uncertain tone. You know I always value your input. Why the hesitation and lack of self-confidence all of a sudden?"

Carla bowed her head. "I wasn't aware that was the case. I'm sorry."

Placing a finger under her partner's chin, Sara raised Carla's head so she could read what was going on in her eyes. "Sweetheart, you know you can talk to me anytime, don't you?"

"What you're really saying is to buck my ideas up and stop feeling sorry for myself, right?"

"No, I'm not saying that at all. You're hurting; we established that back at the station. There's hurting after a relationship has ended and there's doubting your self-worth. I think you're going through the latter and I'm telling you now, that has to stop, right here, right now. For your own sanity, please don't go down that route. No man is worth that."

Carla let out a large sigh and straightened her shoulders. "Thanks for the kick up the arse. I'll address what's going on up here and correct it, I promise." She prodded her forehead.

Sara opened her arms. "Quick hug. I know I don't usually do this; however, I think you need one. Maybe we both need one."

Carla walked into her arms. "Thanks, boss. You're the best. Sorry if I've let you down."

Sara pushed her away. "You haven't and nor will you in the future. Remember, I'm always around, day or night if you need to chat, got that?"

"Thanks, I appreciate it more than you realise."

"Right, setting both our mucky personal lives aside for now, let's see what we can find out from the staff."

CHAPTER 2

BACK AT RECEPTION, the manageress was only too happy to help with Sara's request to view the hotel's footage. They located a perfect shot of the victim as she'd checked in the previous day around five o'clock. The victim's name, according to the register, was Samantha Jordan. When Carla rang Christine back at the station and asked her to run the victim's name and address through the system, surprise, surprise, they turned out to be untraceable. They also found out that the woman had checked in alone.

"She gave a false name and address. Great. That's going to put a kybosh on the investigation before we even get started," Sara complained, thumping her thigh.

"Maybe we should get on to the media right away, show the woman's picture and see if a relative comes forward."

Sighing, Sara agreed. "It's our only option. I'll do that right away." She glanced at the reception desk and caught Nigella Windsor's eye.

The woman walked towards her. "What can I do for you, Inspector?"

"We need to know if the guests in the rooms on either side of the victim's are still at the hotel. If they are, we need to have a word with them before they check out."

"I'll just find out for you." She marched away and swivelled the register to have a look. She returned a few moments later. "Yes, they appear to still be here—by that, I mean they haven't checked out yet."

"Great news. Thanks very much."

The manageress returned to her duties.

"I need to organise getting this woman's image out there. Let me spend the next ten minutes doing that, then we'll go back upstairs and question the guests." Sara rang the people she usually contacted at times such as this, those who represented the local media and told them what she needed.

All of them agreed to air the woman's photo at the earliest opportunity on the lunchtime news. With that chore out of the way, Sara and Carla made their way back up to the fourth floor where the victim's body had been found. Sara knocked on the door to the right first.

A man in his early sixties, grey hair and half-lens spectacles, opened the door. "Hello, can I help?" he asked, sounding nervous.

Sara and Carla produced their IDs. "DI Sara Ramsey and DS Carla Jameson, and you are, sir?"

"James Masterton. What's this about? Oh, wait, what happened next door, I take it? Dreadful situation. I'll be leaving here today. I'm in the middle of packing now. Can't say I feel safe here any longer. I've used this hotel for years and I've never had to deal with anything of this nature before."

"Do you mind if we come in for a moment, Mr Masterton?"

He flung open the door and moved to the centre of the room. His suitcase was lying open on the bed, half full.

"Are you here alone, sir?" Sara asked.

"I am. I'm here on business. It's a convenient hotel, central to where I need to be. I'll be staying elsewhere in the future, take my word on that."

"If you've stayed at the hotel in the past without any incidents occurring, you should give them another chance. This type of thing is a rarity, I assure you."

"That might be the case." He shuddered. "It doesn't sit right with me, though. If I didn't have a meeting to attend around lunchtime just down the road, I would've checked out first thing this morning. Well, after breakfast. I'm too old for this shit, Inspector. I want a quiet life at my age."

"I can understand that. May I ask what you do for a living?"

"I'm a confectionery salesman. I visit the local retailers in the area. The whole of the Midlands really. Never dreamt I'd get caught up in something like this."

"You're hardly caught up in it, unless there's something you need to tell us."

"Like what?" He shook his head frantically. "This has nothing to do with me, if that's what you're suggesting. I didn't even know the woman who got killed. Didn't even see her."

"Okay, calm down, sir. As your room is next to hers, I have to ask if you possibly heard something."

"Are you assuming that or hoping?" he countered.

"Either, sir?" Sara replied, a smile crossing her lips to prevent her from grinding her teeth in annoyance.

"Well, I didn't, not unless you want to know about the raised voices I heard?"

"That's exactly the kind of information we're searching for. What time was that?"

He inhaled a breath that puffed out his cheeks as he thought. "I went down for dinner around eight-fifteen and came back up around nine-thirty. I was about to turn the TV on when I heard a man shouting. It wasn't all the time—intermittent shouting, I'd say."

"Did the lady respond?"

"If she did, I didn't hear her. I prefer not to get involved in other people's domestic squabbles. I had enough of that before I divorced the wife."

"I see. Could you make out any words that were being said?"

"Not really. Possible name-calling perhaps. One word was shouted louder than the rest: slut! Sorry I can't tell you anything further, that's all I've got, I'm afraid."

"That's enough, thank you, sir. We'll need to take a statement down before you leave. Do you have time now?"

He glanced at his watch. "If you can get it down within thirty minutes, then I'm all yours. If not, then no, I don't have time. My customers are used to me being prompt. I'd hate to tarnish my reputation over something that is out of my control, if you get where I'm coming from?"

"I do. Carla, can you take Mr Masterton's statement down while I have a word with the guests in the next room?"

Carla whipped out her notebook and shrugged. "It's all I've got on me, boss."

Sara patted her on the shoulder. "It'll do. Get Mr Masterton to sign it, and then we'll copy it onto the proper statement form when we get back to the station."

She left the room and nipped up the hallway, poking her head into the victim's room as she passed. "Any news for me?"

Lorraine glanced up from examining the woman's body. "I can confirm she didn't have sex before she was murdered."

"Interesting. Maybe the murderer forced her to strip? And her being naked wasn't a voluntary act?"

"Possibly. Who knows?"

Sara pointed at the room next door. "Guest that way heard a man shouting. One word stuck out: *slut*."

Lorraine's mouth turned down at the sides. "Maybe Carla was right. Perhaps she was a prostitute after all."

Sara shook her head. "Not getting that impression myself. I'm going to question the guest on this side now, see what I can glean from them."

"Good luck. Let me know."

"Are you going to be here long?"

"At least another hour or so. Hopefully your mob will have moved the riffraff back several hundred feet by then."

"Backup should be here by now." She left the room and closed the door behind her then knocked on the neighbour's.

A chubby woman with a red glow to her cheeks opened the door.

Sara put her age around the early sixties mark, give or take a few years either side. She produced her ID and introduced herself.

"I've been expecting someone from the police. Do you want to come in? We're packing up to leave."

Sara withdrew her notebook and entered the room. The woman closed the door then sat on the bed next to a man of a similar age. The couple appeared shell-shocked.

"Sorry, can I start by getting your names? Mr and Mrs...?"

"Sampson, Jacqueline and Timothy," the woman volunteered.

"Thank you. I know this has come as a great shock to you both. Would you mind telling me if you overheard anything last night in the room next door?"

The woman slowly shook her head. "I didn't. What about you, love?"

Her husband's head swivelled between his wife and Sara. "No, nothing."

"Okay. Were you in your room all evening?"

"No. We went out for dinner and didn't return until around ten. It was really quiet when we arrived back at the hotel."

"Did you happen to see anyone either enter the room next door or leave?"

"We didn't, I'm sorry. We're not much use to you, are we?"

Sara smiled. "It's fine. The guest on the other side was helpful in that respect. It's not your fault if you weren't in the hotel at the time the incident occurred."

"We'd help if we could," Jaqueline insisted.

"I'm sure you would. I don't suppose you saw the woman who was staying in the room, possibly earlier in the day?"

"I did, as it happens. The chambermaid forgot to leave us any towels. I had to go down to the reception area and ask for some around fiveish. When I got back, the woman was just entering her room. We exchanged hellos, and she shut the door. I continued to my room."

"Was she alone?"

"Oh yes."

"Perhaps you can tell me how she was dressed?"

"In a grey suit. Skirt about knee-length. Very smart she looked, too."

"May I ask why you're both staying here?"

"We're visiting family in the area for a few days. We were due to leave tomorrow but we're checking out today instead. I wouldn't be able to close my eyes tonight, knowing that a beautiful woman lost her life next door last night."

"I can understand that. Where are you from?"

"Meopham in Kent, although we're from Hereford originally, hence our family living in the area."

"What made you leave?"

"We had to go where the work was. Tim has always been the breadwinner in the family, and his job took us to the Kent area. We've moved around down there over the past twenty years. Now that retirement is looming, we're going to look into coming back to this area again. Hereford is in our veins."

"Even after what's happened here in the hotel?"

"Have you seen the news in other areas? It's the same the world over, isn't it? So much anger nowadays. People have forgotten how to control their tempers with devastating effects."

"You're right. I can't say our jobs are getting easier as the years pass. What work do you do, Mr Sampson?"

"It's boring really. I'm in the oil industry, a data analyst. Sounds interesting, but it isn't, I assure you. A good salary is what drives us on."

"Maybe you're right. A lot of people think inspectors are well paid —we're not. I don't do my job for the money, however, luckily for the force. It takes a special kind of person to want to become a police officer."

"I can imagine. I take my hat off to you," the man said, raising an imaginary hat from his head.

"Okay, I'll move on then if you have nothing else for me."

"We haven't. Sorry to let you down, Inspector," Mrs Sampson said, rising from the bed and crossing the large room to the door.

"I'll leave you my card. Should you think of anything else, please ring me. Safe travels back to Kent."

"Thank you," Mrs Sampson said, taking the card and placing it in her blouse pocket.

Sara knocked on a few of the other doors on the opposite side of the corridor, but there was no answer, so she returned to see if Carla had finished with Mr Masterton. She had and was just leaving his room. "All done?"

"Yep, for what it was worth. How did you get on?"

Sara pointed at the room she'd spent the last few minutes in. "Husband and wife team, nothing. That's not quite true. She actually saw the victim entering her room around fiveish, which confirms her time of arrival. I need to look at the hotel footage again, see if we can find her visitor on there."

"I wonder if the receptionist was on duty last night. They quite often work long hours, right?"

Sara frowned. "Let's go. What's your point?"

They made their way back along the corridor to the lift and waited for it to arrive.

"Why don't we look through the footage ourselves to see if we can find her visitor? The receptionist can point out any people who weren't registered at the hotel."

"Excellent thinking. Let's hope she was on duty last night then."

The lift door slid open, and they hopped aboard.

The manageress glanced in their direction as they walked towards the desk. "Any luck?" she asked.

"Yes and no. Can I ask if either you or the receptionist were on duty last night?"

Nigella Windsor shook her head. "No, we both left around six. May I ask why?"

"It was an idea my partner came up with. Would it be possible for us to view the CCTV footage before we leave?"

"Of course. Any reason for that?" Nigella asked, confusion pulling at her brow.

"It would be helpful if we could pinpoint the suspect in your presence. That way, either you or your staff can tell us if the person is a guest at the hotel or a visitor. That would go a long way towards helping the investigation get underway."

"I see. Why don't we go through to my office then? I'll set things up in there."

"Excellent news."

The three of them entered the manageress's office, which was no more than ten by eight. It was a tight squeeze, but hopefully the session would prove to be a fruitful one. Nigella pressed Play on the machine and whizzed through it until someone came into shot. They were twenty minutes through the footage when Sara pointed at the screen.

"There. Can you zoom in on that person? He's entered the hotel and bypassed the reception desk. Do you recognise him as a guest of the hotel, Nigella?"

"No. Although it's hard to tell when he's wearing a hat. Let me see if I can get a better angle on one of the other cameras."

As it turned out, she couldn't.

"Damn. Okay, that leads me to believe he was intentionally trying to disguise himself, knew the cameras would pick him up."

Carla nodded. "I have to agree. Not helpful in the slightest...unless..."

Sara turned to face her. "Go on."

"Unless he parked in the car park, and the cameras outside can pinpoint which car he got out of, and that leads us to his registration number."

Sara raised an eyebrow. "Good thinking. Do you have the other discs for us, Nigella?"

She picked up a couple of cases from the edge of the desk. "All ready for you."

"Thanks. We're going to take them back to the station. You've been super helpful. I'm hoping the pathologist and her team will be finished up there soon. Then you can get back to normality around here."

"Not sure this place will ever be the same again after going through this. Ring me if you need anything else, Inspector."

"I will."

Sara and Carla rushed out of the office and ran down the steps of the hotel to avoid the mob press pack spotting them. A few of the reporters split from the group, eagle-eyed as ever, and chased them to the car. Sara smiled and slipped behind the steering wheel before any of them could come within spitting distance. "That was a close one."

"You're not kidding. What's your gut on this one, boss?"

Sara exited the car park and headed left towards the station. "Too early to say. Maybe she attracted the wrong type of person at work. Was she on some kind of course, a business course?"

"It would explain why she was staying in a hotel. Crap, we're screwed until we can ID the woman, aren't we?"

"You're not wrong there. Either that, or if we can find out more about her killer. Let's not lose faith just yet."

THE SECOND SARA walked into the incident room, she turned on the TV and switched the channel to *Sky News*. Within seconds, the grainy picture of the victim in the hotel lobby filled the screen. Shaking her head, she punched the desk beside her. "What a shit picture that is. I wouldn't bother manning the phones on this one, team. I doubt we're going to be inundated with calls offering up a possible name. I'll be in my office should anyone want me."

Despondent, she bypassed the vending machine and entered her office, stopping momentarily to study the view of the Brecon Beacons in the distance as she always did. Carla knocked on the door, interrupting her reflective spell.

"Want me to start going through the hotel's exterior footage? Are you okay?"

"I'm fine. Ticked off, but that's nothing new at the beginning of a frustrating case, right? If you would. I'll tackle the post and be with you in about an hour."

"Coffee?"

"No, thanks. I'm trying to be good. I've got some water on my desk. I'll have that instead."

"Can't see that lasting long."

Sara chuckled. "Me neither. I heard something on one of those health programmes last night that we should only be drinking two cups of coffee a day."

"I bet you get withdrawal symptoms. Cutting out eighteen cups a day will do that to a person."

Sara scrunched up a blank piece of paper and threw it at her partner. "Oi. I'm not that bad."

Carla left the office and mumbled, "If you say so."

An hour later, and with the paperwork all finished, Sara returned to the incident room. The team had their heads bowed, indicating they were concentrating on the tasks in hand. Carla waved her over.

"Tell me you have something for me?"

"Sorry, I haven't. I have the man entering the hotel. He approached from the road, on foot by the looks of things."

"Damn. That's shot your idea down in flames then."

Carla nodded. "We were pinning our hopes on that. What now?"

Sara held her arms out to the side and dropped them against her thighs as if they were laden with heavy weights. "You tell me. We're stumped until we receive the PM results. Even then I doubt they're going to be able to give us much. The perp didn't have sex with her, so there's going to be a lack of DNA there."

"What about giving the clip showing the man to the media, to run alongside the victim's image?"

Sara cradled her chin between her finger and thumb. "Maybe it's worth a shot. Okay, get me the clearest image you can find, and I'll send it to my contacts again."

Carla pointed at the screen. "This is the best one I could source. Want to go with that?"

"Yep. Print it off for me. I'll take a photo of the screen as well. They can decide which of them to use. These damn images look so different once they're on the TV screen."

Carla printed it off and handed the copy to Sara. She took a photo of the image on the screen using her phone and proceeded to send it to her contacts. "Done. Now all we have to do is sit back and wait."

"Want me to start on something else? Tying up the loose ends on the two previous cases we solved?"

"Makes sense."

Sara went into her office again and closed the door. When things got bad, she had a habit of reaching out to Mark, whom she'd grown close to over the past few months.

"Can you talk?"

"For a few minutes. We have a lull between patients. What's up?" he asked, sounding pleased she'd rung.

"Nothing. Slow investigation, so I thought I'd give you a ring and invite you over for dinner tonight. That is if you're not too busy."

"Hmm...let me check my diary."

A familiar knot formed in her stomach as the thought of him letting her down struck.

"Yep, looks like I'm free. Well, there was this one young lady who slipped her phone number in my pocket earlier, but she seemed the stalkerish type. I've decided to swerve that one and stick with the one I've already got."

Sara laughed. "I'm honoured. Shame on the girl for doing that. Maybe she thinks having a vet for a boyfriend would be a thrill. I could put her right on that one."

"I'm sure you could. I'm pretty dull, aren't I?"

"I wouldn't say that. Maybe to other girls you would be, but I'm hardly an exciting catch myself. Anyway, what do you fancy?"

"Apart from you between two slices of bread, nothing much."

"You're hilarious. What about a piece of steak with all the trim-mings? Are you up for that?"

"Sounds perfect. I'll stop by the off-licence and grab a bottle of red as my contribution, how's that?"

"Great stuff. I'll be home slightly later than normal then. I'll need to drop into the supermarket on the way home. Not that it matters to you; you won't be there until about eight-thirty, yes?"

"Yep, I have an operation to do at six. I should be finished around seven forty-five, by the time I've cleaned up and closed the surgery."

"Good. I'll see you then."

"Looking forward to it more than you know. Cheeky question: am I staying over?"

Her cheeks warmed. "Do you want to?"

"What do you think?"

"Then I suppose you're stopping the night. See you later."

"Bye for now."

She ended the call sporting a huge smile. It might have taken her two years to come to terms with Philip's death before she even considered dating again, but now she had no regrets dropping her barrier or letting Mark persuade her to go out with him. Not that they went out much. They were both on an even keel there, in that they both preferred to put their feet up and chill out in front of the TV at the end of a long day. She was too old to start dating from scratch, going to nightclubs to see which mate she could attract. Mark was one of the nicest people she'd ever met. Kind, considerate and always had a smile on his face, even when things were stacked against him. She was lucky to have him in her life. She adored him.

THE AFTERNOON DRAGGED PAST. Sara announced the team should go home and get some rest before the investigation really took off. They walked to their respective cars. "There's a lightness in your step. I'm thinking you're on a promise this evening."

Sara smiled and jabbed Carla in the arm. "I think so. I'm stopping off at the supermarket for supplies. Thought I'd treat us to a nice piece of steak."

"Sounds delicious. Enjoy your evening," Carla said sadly, her head dropping slightly.

Sara rubbed her arm. "You'll find someone new soon, love. A pretty girl like you is sure to attract the right sort of man eventually. Hey, if I can do it, then the odds are stacked in your favour."

"It's too soon. Yes, I'm lonely, but on the other hand, my heart has to heal first. It's well and truly damaged right now."

"It'll pass. I promise you. And, yes, that's the voice of experience talking. I swore I'd never let another man get under my skin once I lost Philip, but Mark has managed to do just that. Give it time."

"I will. Hey, don't go worrying about me, enjoy your evening. See you in the morning."

Sara sat in her car and watched her partner drive out ahead of her, her heart aching for Carla and the misery she was going through. Andrew was a bastard for letting her down the way he had.

After calling in at Morrisons, she drove the rest of the way home singing along to the new love songs album she'd purchased the week before. As usual, her apprehension grew as she approached her house. The recent attempts to vandalise her new home had left a deep scar that was taking longer than expected to heal. A quick scan of the front of the house, and everything seemed fine. She parked on the drive, collected the bags of groceries and walked up the front path. Unlocking the door, she placed the bags on the floor and swept Misty into her arms and kicked the door closed behind her.

"Hello, munchkin. Have you had a good day?"

Misty purred and rubbed her head under Sara's chin.

"Go on, on the floor. I have a meal to prepare. I bet you're hungry, too."

Misty followed her into the kitchen. After feeding her moggy, Sara let Misty out of the back door and waited for her to return. Then she peeled the potatoes, prepared the steak with a special steak seasoning she'd bought and chopped up some mushrooms. She added a sliced tomato and opened a can of sweetcorn. Pleased with her efforts, she bolted upstairs and slipped on her leisure outfit.

Noting the time on the clock beside her bed, she rushed back downstairs and switched on the oven to cook the chips.

Mark arrived at eight-twenty with an expensive bottle of red wine.

"You shouldn't have. This must have cost you a bomb."

He bent down and kissed her on the lips. "You're worth it. It smells delicious. Can I help?"

"It's all in hand. Can you lay the table or would you rather eat in the living room in front of the TV?"

He grinned. "You know me so well. I'll set up the trays instead. I'm looking forward to this. I haven't had a steak in a while."

"We both deserve a treat. I hope I don't spoil it. Never really had much luck cooking steak in the past."

"Want me to do it for you? I've had my fair share of practice on the barbeque."

"We'll do it together."

They giggled like children while they cooked the meal. Mark told her tales of his time as a vet, through his studying time at college up to the present day. "You'd be surprised the lengths owners are prepared to go to in order to pamper their pets. One of my clients even built a full-sized pool in their front garden because their back garden was too small for their ageing Labrador who was riddled with arthritis, all because I'd recommended they book the dog in for a hydrotherapy session or two."

"No. That must have cost them a pretty penny."

"Yep, around twenty grand, I believe. According to the owner, it was worth every penny to see her dog pain free."

"I suppose hearing stories like that is better than having an abandoned, abused pooch turn up at the surgery."

"Sure does. It takes a certain type of person to raise their hands to an animal. Thankfully, I don't have to deal with many cases in this area. That's not to say it doesn't go on, though."

The conversation had become serious between them. Sara set out to lighten the mood again. "Well, if I'm not mistaken, I think our meal is ready and, miracle upon miracles, I didn't ruin the steak."

"I think I had a hand in that."

She kissed him and served up the meal. The evening flew past after that, and they retired to bed at around eleven.

It felt good going to bed with a man again, not just for the sex, but having someone to snuggle up to on chilly evenings was something to savour.

CHAPTER 3

SHE HAD COME downstairs before him and was checking their cars weren't damaged from the safety of the lounge window when Mark crept up behind her and almost scared her to death.

"What are you doing?" he asked, resting his chin on her shoulder.

Her heart raced faster than a runaway train. "Nothing, just pulling the curtains and seeing if my neighbours, Ted and Mavis, were up and about yet. That reminds me…when the nice weather comes around, I've promised to invite them over for a dinner."

"You have? Any specific reason why?"

Me and my big mouth! Ted was the one who'd repaired most of the damage caused by the vandalism which had occurred while Mark had been away on one of his courses. That way, she'd managed to keep what had happened from him. "No reason. We got chatting one day, and I like them. Found out they lost their daughter last year while she was on a backpacking holiday in Australia."

"How sad. Did she have an accident?"

Sara turned in his arms to face him. "No, she was murdered. They feel guilty for allowing her to travel alone."

"How dreadful. They're going to live with that guilt for years to come. Life's so cruel, isn't it?"

"Desperately so at times."

He cringed. "Sorry. Has it brought back memories you'd rather forget?"

She shrugged and sighed. "The memories are always there. Certain things shift them from the little room at the back of my mind now and again. Hey, I'm getting there. Now I have you in my life, everything is getting far easier to deal with. We'd better get a wriggle on or we're both going to be late."

He kissed the tip of her nose. "I'm always here if you ever need to chat, you know that, yes?"

"I do. I'll shout if things ever get too much that I can't cope with them."

She flew around for the next ten minutes ensuring Misty's needs were met by cleaning out her litter tray and feeding her before she grabbed her coat. She and Mark left the house together. Ted walked across the road with his poodle, Muffin. He made a beeline for Sara. She smiled, hoping he wouldn't mention the trouble she'd been through while Mark was in earshot. He didn't.

"Nice to see you again, Sara. Are you well?"

"Very, Ted. What about you and Mavis?"

"We're surviving. Busy pottering around in the garden now the days are warming up."

"How wonderful. Feel free to have a go at mine if you get bored." She laughed.

Ted smiled and waved. "You know you've only got to say the word and I'll help out in a shot."

"I know. Hey, I haven't forgotten I promised to cook you a meal either. I mentioned to Mark last night over dinner, didn't I?" she called over as Mark was getting in his car.

"She did that. Nice to meet you, Ted. Sorry, I've got to go. The surgery won't open itself."

They watched him start the car and drive away.

Sara faced Ted. "I'm so glad you didn't mention the vandalism. My heart was in my mouth in case you said anything."

Ted frowned. "Don't tell me you haven't told the lad?"

She sighed. "I didn't want to scare him off. The damage to his car was enough for him to contend with."

Ted's expression was one of anger. He wagged a finger at her. "Don't keep him in the dark, love. Secrets like that have a habit of coming out and biting you in the arse. Oops...excuse the language."

She leant forward and pecked him on the cheek. "I know you mean well. I'll consider telling him when the time is right, I promise. Gotta fly. Give my love to Mavis."

"I will. Think about what I said and take care."

"Okay, you win. Gosh, it's like having another father around." She chuckled and jumped in the car.

"I'll take that as a compliment," Ted said, waving her off and then shaking Muffin's lead to get walking again.

Sara drove past her neighbour and smiled. She switched the CD on and relaxed during the drive into the city. It wasn't long before she joined the large queue that leaving home ten minutes earlier could have avoided. She rang Carla at the station. "Sorry, I'm caught in traffic. Just warning you in case the chief comes looking for me. Any news?"

"Not really. Where are you?"

"Just coming up to Holmer Road. Not far."

"Drive carefully. See you soon."

Sara ended the call and rested against the headrest, her mind drifting back to the lovely evening she'd shared with Mark, and she found herself wondering if she was finally getting closer to him. Daft question to ask when she already knew the answer. She was, and she wasn't sure how she felt about that in all honesty. The traffic crawled along. She kept an eye on the car behind her. The driver kept inching forward even when she wasn't moving. "Back off, jerk. There's like a thousand cars ahead of me. No need to keep hounding me, dickhead."

The man was young, and he had a goatee beard and large black-tinted sunglasses even though the sun wasn't shining, which she thought was strange. Her suspicious gene prodded her, warning her to be careful. What if he was one of the gang members sent from

Liverpool to intentionally disrupt her life? *Don't be so ridiculous, he's just an impatient guy waiting in the queue, nothing sinister about that.*

Fifteen minutes later, she drove into her parking space. She left the car and inhaled a large breath of fresh air after all the stale air she'd been forced to consume inside the car. Jeff had a cheerful smile waiting for her when she opened the door to the main entrance.

"Morning, boss. Got caught up in the traffic, did you?"

She nodded. "You could say that. Is it getting worse out there, or is it only me it seems to affect?"

"Definitely getting worse, boss. I've taken to leaving at least thirty minutes earlier nowadays."

"I usually do. One of my neighbours started chatting, you know how it is. All quiet overnight?"

"Yep, nothing to report."

"Not sure how I feel about that. Thankful that I don't have to contend with much first thing other than the dreaded paperwork, but, then again, we need the information to start coming in on the Jane Doe if we're going to solve her murder quickly. You know how I hate these types of crimes lingering. The families have a right to justice. The sooner we give them that, the happier I am about the investigation."

"I think we all feel the same, boss."

"I know. Better get on as I'm running late. Ring me if anything interesting drops in your lap."

"You've got it, ma'am."

Sara ascended the stairs, her gaze fixed in front of her. When she got to the top step, she bumped into DCI Carol Price. "Damn, you caught me arriving late. I'll work longer this evening to make up for it, I promise," she waffled, her cheeks heating up.

"You'll do no such thing. The amount of hours you put in around here, I'm hardly going to come down heavy on you when you're a few minutes late one day. Is everything all right? I'm free for a while if you need a chat."

"I'm fine. Left home a few minutes later than usual and got caught in the damn traffic, that's all."

The chief scrutinised her, checking for any sign of her lying, she presumed.

"There's no need for you to peer into my soul like that. It's the truth, I promise you."

"All right. If you're sure. You know how much I worry about you after what you've been through lately."

"I know. You'll be the first one I run to if things get out of hand, you have my word on that." Her gaze drifted off to the left—she couldn't help it. A professional interrogator would have instantly picked up that she was lying. Yes, she had eventually informed the chief about the vandalism issues she'd dealt with; however, what she'd neglected to tell her was that she'd heard from the officer in charge of her husband's case and he'd issued her a warning about a likely threat awaiting her in the near future. Sara was the type who preferred to deal with cold, hard facts, not hearsay.

"Make sure I am. Walk with me." They headed towards the incident room side by side. "What about this latest case? I hear on the grapevine it's already causing you a lot of frustration."

Sara pushed through the door. "Nothing more than usual with this type of case, ma'am. The victim is marked as a Jane Doe at present. We're working hard on trying to find an ID for her but failing every way we turn."

"I saw the TV appeal go out last night. Something is bound to come of that."

Sara shrugged. "You'd think so, but nothing has come in so far, according to the desk sergeant anyway. That leads me to think she's either not from this area, which is a distinct possibility, especially as she was staying at the hotel, or she has no living relatives or friends, which seems unlikely."

"Hmm...if I were pushed, I'd be inclined to think the former as well if that's all you have. What's next on your agenda?"

"Next step is to see what Lorraine finds for us—sorry, she's the pathologist dealing with the victim."

"I knew who you meant. What's the likelihood of anything coming from that?"

She sighed. "I'm not holding my breath. Although the victim was found naked, Lorraine did a preliminary examination at the scene and confirmed the woman hadn't had sex. Therefore, we won't have a DNA trail to follow."

"Crap, I can see why it's so frustrating for you."

Sara turned to address the team. "Morning all. Anything come to light yet?" The team either mumbled a disappointing no or shook their heads in response. "Okay, let's crack on. Dig deeper and work smarter. Someone knows who this woman is. We need to try and locate that someone." Sara's mobile tinkled that she'd received a text. She withdrew it from her pocket and viewed the message. Her heart stopped for a brief second and then beat erratically as she read the message.

You've been warned. Now we're coming to get you.

SHE STUMBLED into a nearby desk as her legs gave way. DCI Price grabbed her arm to prevent her from falling. "Get a chair, quickly," she shouted.

Barry was already on his feet. He dragged the chair out from behind the closest desk and helped to lower Sara into it.

Stunned, she tried to gather her poise swiftly. "Oh dear, I don't know what came over me."

DCI Price snatched the phone out of her hand and read the message. "What the fuck? You," she said, pointing at Barry. "Take DI Ramsey into her office. Carla, can you bring two coffees in, please. Mine's black with one sugar."

Carla scraped her chair and rushed to the vending machine.

Barry placed his arm under Sara's and guided her through to her office where he deposited her in her chair. "Are you all right, boss?" Concern was etched into his features.

Sara tried to give him a reassuring smile but failed and nodded instead.

"Leave us alone," DCI Price ordered, harsher than was necessary, sending Barry scuttling out of the room. "Wait. I'm sorry for snapping."

Barry accepted the chief's apology and rushed out of the room.

Carla entered carrying two cups of coffee. "Was it another message?"

DCI Price stared at Carla. "What's going on? I demand to know."

Sara was in shock, unable to form any words, so Carla filled the DCI in.

DCI Price growled, her annoyance clearly bubbling to the surface. "Bloody hell. What have I told you about keeping things of this magnitude from me? Carla, leave us alone please."

Carla backed out of the room, her gaze locking with Sara's as she sent a silent apology. Sara closed her eyes, aware of the rollicking heading her way.

DCI Price flung herself into the chair opposite her and picked up her coffee. She blew on it for a few seconds, avoiding eye contact with Sara before she sipped at her drink.

"I'm sorry," Sara said, her voice childlike, as if she was anticipating the chief tearing into her.

Instead, DCI Price glanced her way and shook her head. "As usual, you're misreading the signs. When have I ever come down heavy on you? Never—not to my knowledge anyway. Jesus, all I ask is that you include me in things of this nature. Tell me this: if I hadn't been in the room when you received that message, would you have informed me about it? And don't lie. Actually, I'll answer for you. No, you bloody wouldn't, otherwise you would have told me about the others. The *others* Carla was referring to, if I'm not mistaken. Shit, what a frigging mess."

Sara was tempted to apologise again but stopped herself knowing what the chief's likely reaction would be. She swallowed down the bile that had settled in the back of her throat. All she wanted to do was curl up in a ball until they caught the bastards who were intent on wrecking her life.

"Talk to me, for fuck's sake. I'm not a damn ogre. Stop treating me like one and spill."

Sara cleared her throat and thrust her shoulders back. "What can I say? After I solved my last case, I was relaxing in the bath when I received a call from the detective dealing with my husband's case in Liverpool." She paused to take a breath and to calm her racing heart as an unnerving motion hit her chest.

"Go on. Take a sip of coffee. I've got all the time in the world to listen. Take advantage of that fact and tell me everything. You need to get this out in the open. Look at you, for Christ's sake, you're a wreck."

Sara took several sips of her coffee that was now cool enough to drink. Then she inhaled and exhaled a few steadying breaths. "DI Smart informed me that his team had arrested the gang leader who shot Philip."

DCI Price punched the air. "That's good news. Why aren't you leaping around in jubilation?"

"Because the good news came with a warning attached."

"Which was? Crap, it's like waiting for an old chicken to lay her final egg."

Sara smiled at the analogy, they both did, breaking the icy atmosphere. "Smart told me that in other cases, once the leader of a gang was in custody, the other members struck out, targeting the victim's family. I guess that means me. Since then I've received numerous texts, the threatening kind that I've learnt to discount as soon as I've got them. You won't get a trace on the text, so don't even bother. They're devious; they'll be using burner phones to twist the screw. I haven't let the other texts affect me, not sure why I let this specific one get to me. I feel kind of foolish now."

"Why? This is dangerous stuff, Sara. We need to treat this seriously from the outset. Not to put too fine a point on it, but I think your life is in genuine danger. We need to ensure these people don't get near you."

"How? I'll be buggered if I'm going to go into hiding, ma'am."

"I'll need to think about the whys and wherefores and get back to you. Do you have an alarm fitted in your house?"

"No. Is that truly necessary? Those things have a habit of going off regularly. The last thing I want to do is start driving my neighbours potty. I have a security camera fitted over the front door, won't that suffice?"

"I doubt it. Get one fitted at the rear of the property, too, and that might satisfy me a little. I still think you should install an alarm, though."

"I'll fit the camera but not the alarm. I think you're overreacting a touch."

DCI Price's eyebrows rose. "Really, after the way you reacted when you received that text? I don't think so. I don't want to fall out about this, Sara. Your safety is paramount, are you hearing me?"

"I am. I'm sure it's just idle threats."

"I'd love to tell you you're right; however, I think the opposite is true. I don't want you going anywhere alone, got that?"

"I won't, you have my word."

DCI Price went to stand and then flopped back into her chair. "Tell me, what does your new fella say about all this?" She leant forward, linked her hands together and placed them on the desk. "And don't bother lying, I can tell when you do."

"He doesn't know. I don't want him involved. Actually, I think I'm going to give him a call right now and tell him we're over."

"*What? Why?* I thought you two were getting on well together."

"We are. My aim is to keep him out of harm's way. Bloody hell, he's already had his car stripped of paint by these thugs, and that was when they were issuing warnings, not threats. Can you imagine what they'll do to him if they up their game? No, I'd rather not take the risk. In fact, if this conversation is finished, I'm going to do it now."

DCI Price tutted and rose from her seat. This time she made it all the way to the door. "I think you're making a grave mistake by ditching him, especially if you have feelings for him."

Sara's eyes misted up. "I'll feel better this way."

DCI Price opened the door. "I'll leave you to it. If *anything* out of the ordinary happens, either while you're on duty or when you're at home, ring me immediately. That's an order, not a request, by the way."

Sara swallowed hard and nodded. "I will. I promise." She watched the chief close the door gently behind her as she left the room and heaved out a sigh full of anxiety and trepidation. *Please forgive me for what I'm about to do, Mark. It's truly for the best, although I can't explain my reasons for doing it now. I will in the future, if you're still speaking to me.*

She gulped a few times and then, with a shaking hand, she rang his number. He answered the phone with the usual smile in his voice which cut her in two.

"Hello, you. Did you forget to tell me something this morning?"

"In a way. Please listen to me and don't interrupt."

"Sounds ominous. Is everything all right, Sara?"

"No, it isn't. I'm sorry, Mark. I've tried so hard to make this work between us, but it just isn't."

"Whoa! Sara, what the hell are you talking about? You want to break up? I can't believe this. Why?"

"I don't really want to go into detail, Mark. Please don't make this harder than it needs to be. We're finished. Thank you for trying to mend my broken heart."

"Don't. Wait! Don't you dare hang up on me. If you do, I'll come down there and make a nuisance of myself." His tone was one of desperation.

Her slightly mended heart shattered into tiny pieces. She felt such a bitch doing this to one of the nicest men she knew, but there really wasn't an alternative if she was determined to keep him safe. "I'm warning you, come down here and I'll have you arrested for harassment."

"Seriously? I go from sharing your bed one minute to being officially warned off in your capacity as an inspector. I don't get it. I deserve to know what I've done wrong. Because I'm struggling to fathom that out at this moment. I thought we'd overcome all the obstacles in our way. Jesus, Sara. I *love* you!"

She gasped. It was the first time he'd ever told her that, which only made her feel a thousand times worse. "I'm sorry. I've been living a lie the past few months, Mark. I refuse to do it any longer." There was an edge to her voice, shocking even her. "I hope you find someone worthy of you and the love you can give them in the near future. Goodbye."

"Sara...don't do this...plea—"

She ended the call before he could say anything further and broke down in tears. That had to be the worst phone call she'd ever had to make in her entire life. *What an utter bitch I am! To throw away my one true chance of happiness.* Her professional self took control. If she didn't end it with him now, this time next week he could be lying on the slab at the mortuary. She grabbed a tissue from the packet lying in the top drawer of her desk and sobbed. She was crying that hard she neglected to hear Carla enter the room. The first she knew of her presence was when Carla slung an arm around her shoulder. Sara almost launched into outer space.

"Hey, what's wrong?" Carla asked, taking a few steps back out of her personal space.

Sara rubbed at her eyes with the tissue and pulled another from the packet to blow her nose. "Damn, you shouldn't see me like this. I'm supposed to set an example. How are you going to see me as your fearless leader when I'm a snivelling idiot?"

"You're human. If anything, I respect you more when you're open like this. Is this because of the text you were sent?"

"Yes and no. I hate the thought of being out of my depth, you know that. I'm drowning, sinking fast, Carla, I admit that."

"Nonsense. I've never met a stronger person than you. Bloody hell, I break up with my boyfriend and I lose it big time. You say goodbye to your husband, and your determination gets you back on track within a few months."

She sobbed again when Carla mentioned breaking up with her boyfriend. After a few fractious moments, she raised her head and looked Carla in the eye. "I've joined the club."

Her partner frowned. "What club?"

"The breaking-up-with-my-boyfriend club."

Carla's eyes widened, and her mouth dropped open. Recovering a few seconds later, she demanded, "What are you talking about? You and Mark were getting on famously from what I saw outside the station a few weeks ago."

She was referring to when Mark had reported the vandalism on his car and Carla had been spying on them while they'd shared a kiss outside. She sobbed, remembering that kiss. *Jesus, I need to get a grip.* As if someone had waved a magic wand over her, she blew her nose, dabbed her eyes dry and sat at her desk as if the past five minutes hadn't happened. "I'm fine. Back to work."

Carla walked around the other side of the desk and stared long and hard at her. "You're kidding me. I need to know the ins and outs. You can't leave me dangling like this, that would be grossly unfair."

"Grossly unfair or not, I need to get my mind off this, and quickly. So, no dilly-dallying, let's get back to work. I'll sort through the usual dross and be with you in half an hour. I'm a professional, Carla, and need work to occupy my mind."

Her mobile jingled that a text message had arrived. Both she and Carla stared at the phone. Sara picked it up and read the message, the breath she'd been holding on to seeping through her parted lips. It was from Mark.

My sweetest, Sara. Don't do this. I meant what I said, I love you. I won't be able to live without you. Fact. Call me tonight when you get home, please?

SHE PLACED the phone back on the desk, harder than she'd intended.

"Don't keep me in suspense. Who was it from?"

Sara glanced up at her partner. "My ex. Leave it, Carla. What's done is done. It was wrong for me to get involved so soon after Philip's death, I realise that now."

Carla made a guttural noise that sounded like a growl. "You're wrong, not only in what you're saying, but for dumping him. He was good for you. We've all seen a change in you around the office since you started seeing him. I can't figure you out."

"Good. I prefer to have a bit of mystery surrounding me." Sara smiled, hoping her attempt at humour paid off and Carla would give up hounding her.

Carla stamped her foot and, without saying anything further, scowled at her and left the room.

Once the door closed, Sara contemplated what was going on in her life and how she could overcome it. The latter part was beyond her. How could she battle the unseen? If the gang was about to strike, she didn't have a clue how or when that was likely to be. At least Mark would be safe now. That in itself would be a blessed relief when everything kicked off as she anticipated it would do. She chewed on her lip.

What if the gang comes after me and I'm out with Carla? What then? How can I protect her? The chief has insisted I shouldn't go out there alone, not that I would. But shit, Carla will be in the firing line along with me... unless I swap partners for the foreseeable future and take one of the men with me. Would that work? Would it be fair choosing someone on the team with the intention of making them a prime target?

It was a dilemma she could do without on top of everything else that had happened.

Bring it on, bastards, I'm ready and waiting for you. If you mow me down then so be it; it means I'll join the love of my life sooner than anticipated.

Mark's face filled her mind. She was wrong to have ever got involved with him, she knew that now, and no matter how much she adored him, she struggled to figure out if those feelings transmitted into love.

CHAPTER 4

AFTER TACKLING her paperwork and managing to ignore another three messages from Mark, pleading with her to reconsider, Sara rejoined the team in the incident room. The group all turned her way, concern written on their faces. She waved a hand in front of her. "I'm fine. Life goes on, folks, and we have a murderer to find. What have we got so far, anything?"

Carla was the first to speak. "Nothing has come in from either the TV or radio appeals. Would it be worth chasing them up, see if they had any calls at their end?"

"Might be worth a shot. I'm truly disappointed by the results so far. Actually, let me do the ringing around. I'll see if any of my contacts can suggest someone I can ring to see if we can go national on this, just in case she's not from this area, which is probably the likely scenario."

"I agree. Is there anything else we can be doing in the meantime?"

"Nothing. Not until we hear back from Lorraine. Yes, ring her, it wouldn't hurt to chase the PM up. Hopefully she can give us something to sink our teeth into. If not, I haven't got a frigging clue where to turn next." She clicked her fingers. "Wrong assumption. Jill, will you pop up and see Maddy Powell in Missing Persons for me? Take a copy of the victim's photo and try to match it to anyone reported missing in the last twenty-four hours. I know it's a long shot, but it's all we've got at the moment." She nipped back into the office and sent Jill the image which she printed off and took upstairs with her.

Sara walked over to the whiteboard and jotted down a few questions and facts that were niggling her. Starting with the man: why was he on foot? Where had he come from to meet up with the victim? Was he local? Then she moved on to the victim, name unknown. Was she here on business as her attire hung in the wardrobe suggested? If so, what type of business was she in? Was the man a colleague? Were they having a secret office affair? Why did she feel the need to book into the hotel under an assumed name? Where did she live? And where was her ID? Did the man take it with the intention to fool the police? There were far too many questions rolling around in her mind, and no, not one solitary answer to get the investigation underway.

Jill seemed dejected when she reentered the room an hour later. "Nothing, boss."

"That just about sums this case up. Okay, let's keep digging, guys. I've managed to persuade the national press and TV news to run the story later today. Hopefully we'll be inundated with calls to deal with tomorrow."

"Dare I ask what happens if we're not?" Carla asked.

Sara shrugged. "You tell me, because I'm at a loss to bloody know. A couple more hours, guys, and then we'll call it a day."

She wandered into her office and sat behind her desk. She massaged her temples, fearing a headache was brewing, and stared at her phone as if expecting it to tinkle a new text had arrived from Mark. His other texts had almost broken her heart. He was pleading with her not to give up on them. To rethink her decision. To tell him what he'd done wrong to damage their relationship. She couldn't supply him with the answers. She had to get on with her life without him, at least until the team up in Liverpool tracked down the rest of the gang intent on destroying her.

· · ·

THE MIND-NUMBING and disappointing afternoon dragged past. The team said their farewells and left the station together in a pack.

"Want to stop off at the pub for a quick one?" Barry suggested.

"I'll take a rain check, if you don't mind," Sara said, a glimmer of a smile tugging at her lips.

The others seemed disheartened by her turning them down and walked across the road to the pub. She watched them with a heavy heart, knowing she was in for a very lonely evening. *Don't think that. I have Misty to snuggle up to.*

She drove home, the night getting darker by the time she arrived at the house. She groaned. Mark's car was parked outside her house.

Damn, just what I don't need.

She parked on her driveway and walked back to the front door. Upon further inspection, she realised that Mark wasn't in his vehicle. She turned around, scanning the small close—there was nowhere for him to hide. Maybe one of the neighbours had taken pity on him and had invited him in. She took a punt and trotted across the road to Ted and Mavis's house to see if he was there.

Ted opened the door with his usual warm smile. "Hello, love. Everything all right, is it?"

"I'm looking for Mark. I don't suppose he's here with you, is he?"

"No. We saw him pull up about half an hour ago. The two gentlemen in the car already parked outside your house got out of their vehicle, and he followed them to their car. They took off then. I presumed they were all going to meet up with you down the pub."

Sara's breath caught in her throat while she listened to Ted. *Shit, damn and blast! Two men! Don't tell me they've abducted him. Please, not that.* Plastering a smile on her face, she said, "Must have been Warren and Luke. Cheeky beggars. I told them to meet me here."

Ted sighed, looking relieved. "Thought something drastic had gone on there. For a moment you drifted off as if the situation was a bad one."

Sara jabbed a finger at her temple. "Just my mind playing tricks on me after a long day at work. I'm sure they'll return soon. I'd better sort out some food for when they come back. Sorry to disturb you, Ted. Say hi to Mavis for me."

"I will, love. Have a good evening."

"You, too."

She turned and walked back towards her house, her legs stiff as if lead weights were anchored to her calves. Her heart rate escalated the closer she got to Mark's car. Using the torch on her phone, she peered in through the driver's window and spotted a note on the front seat. She lifted the handle, and the door sprang open. Taking a glove from her jacket pocket, she picked up the note and read it.

No harm will come to him as long as you do as we say. We'll be in touch soon.

HER PANIC GENE TOOK OVER. She had to reprimand herself to remain calm. She thrust the note in her pocket and slammed the car door. Sara entered the house, and Misty was soon blazing an ominous trail around her ankles. She picked up her cat, buried her head in the comfort of her fur and sobbed. She remained in the same position for what seemed like twenty minutes when in reality it was probably only a few. She'd never felt so helpless in all her thirty-two years in this world.

Her phone rang. She hurriedly placed Misty on the floor and answered it. "Hello. Who is this?"

"Dumb question, Mrs Cop. You know damn well who this is. You want to see your fella again...alive?"

"Please, please, don't hurt him. I'm prepared to do anything you want me to do, just don't hurt him."

"First of all, you tell anyone we've got him, and we'll kill him. Got that? You're on your own."

She exhaled a breath that was constricting her chest. "I've got it. Tell me what you need?"

"All in good time. We'll keep your fella in a safe place for now. We're watching your every move. Don't take us for idiots."

"I won't. I promise. Please, don't hurt him. He doesn't deserve this."

Mark's screaming filled the line. Then the phone went dead.

Sara collapsed to the floor. Misty jumped on her lap. She clung to her cat, gripping her tightly until Misty tried to escape her grasp. "I'm sorry, baby. Oh God. What do I do now? They've warned me not to tell anyone. I don't think I can do that, but if I do, they'll probably kill him."

Releasing Misty, she pulled herself up using the handle on the lounge door. Desperate for something to help calm her nerves, she opened the bottle of whisky she had left over from Christmas and poured herself half a glass. After downing a good measure, she fell onto the sofa and stayed there in the dark for the next hour or so, contemplating what she should do next. This wasn't her field of expertise, and she was struggling with how to put things right. Of course, she couldn't do that until the people holding Mark gave her further instructions.

Finally, after different worrying scenarios played out in her mind, Sara let Misty out of the back door and waited for her to return. Then she locked every door and checked all the windows were secured in the house and went upstairs to bed. Her bones were weary, and her head was pounding even more than it had been in the office that afternoon when her headache had set in.

She climbed into bed, fully clothed, and was asleep in no time, only to wake a little while later when the nightmares began. All of them consisted of Mark sitting in the dark somewhere, tied to a chair with a gag in his mouth. She peered closer. Pain swam in his eyes. She inspected his body. Blood spatter had splashed his denim shirt—his favourite shirt.

Sara jolted awake, not wanting to know where the blood had come from. She reached for Misty again and held her tight as she drifted off to sleep for the umpteenth time. The alarm woke her out of her deep sleep at seven a.m. Kicking back the quilt, she rushed into the bathroom to shower. Her stomach grumbled, complaining of its lack of food in the last eighteen hours. She'd only managed to grab a sand-wich at lunchtime and couldn't bear to face anything the night before. Her mind was busy concentrating on other things, such as what was going on with Mark and whether he had the strength of character to overcome anything the gang members likely threw at him. *Of course he won't be able to deal with the pain. He's a vet, for God's sake, not a hardened police officer like me. Damn, why did they have to involve him in this? Why?*

CHAPTER 5

SARA DROVE into work on autopilot, leaving as soon as she'd had her shower and dressed in her navy skirt suit. Her stomach rejected the piece of toast she'd tried to shove down her neck. She tipped away her half-drunk coffee, threw the uneaten slice of toast and marmalade in the bin and set off.

She hit the steering wheel with the heel of her hand when she realised she hadn't cleaned Misty's tray out before leaving the house. *I'm too hard on myself. One day won't hurt.* She'd give Misty an extra treat when she arrived home this evening to compensate for her mistake.

The station appeared in her sightline ahead at the same time her phone rang. "Hello," she said tentatively.

"Hi, it's me. Are you going to be long?"

Sara blew out a relieved breath when her partner's voice rippled down the line. "Two minutes. What's up?"

"We've got another body that we should look into."

"Goddammit! Grab the address and meet me outside. There's no point in me dragging myself all the way upstairs if we're going to leave a few minutes later."

"Got ya. I hope you haven't had a greasy fry-up this morning. It's a gruesome one."

"Great. No, my appetite was non-existent this morning, thankfully."

"See you soon."

Sara pulled into the car park and quickly checked her appearance in the mirror while she waited for Carla to join her. She'd used heavier makeup to disguise her restless night and the trauma of the nightmares she'd endured.

Carla waved and rushed towards the car.

"Hi, how are you this morning?" Sara asked, trying to keep her voice cheerful.

"I was fine when I showed up for work. Not feeling so good now I know what's in store for us."

"Sounds gross. Okay, where are we heading?"

"Credenhill Park Wood. I can direct you."

"I've heard of it, just can't place it."

"Turn left at the top and keep going until I tell you to stop. I used to take our dog up there when I was younger and still living at home. It's a pretty steep climb to get to the top."

"Super, just what we need first thing in the morning."

Carla chuckled. "What's the matter, don't you have much energy left after a night in the sack with Mark?"

Sara sharply turned to face her partner. "No. You couldn't be further from the truth. Mark didn't stay over last night. Don't presume to think you know everything about my life, Carla."

"Whoa! Sorry, I was only having a laugh. Didn't mean to cause any offence."

Sara briefly closed her eyes and chastised herself. "My fault. Actually, it's not my fault, and yes, you're guilty of being insensitive because you know full well we split up yesterday."

Carla thumped her leg, hard. "Shit, so you did. I suppose I'm so consumed with my own life at present that I neglected to think about that. Can we start the morning over again?"

Sara cracked a smile. "Deal. How was your evening?"

"Boring, uneventful, dire. They all amount to the same thing, right? How was yours?"

Full of drama, traumatic, anything but uneventful. "About the same as yours," she lied.

Two minutes later, they arrived in Credenhill and turned up a small track. "Are you sure this is the right way?" Sara asked, concerned.

"Yes, it'll open out soon into a small car park. I think it's cute having the place tucked away like this. It means less visitors to battle your way through."

"I suppose." Sara nodded and continued to drive down the pot-filled lane and was relieved when the road widened and the car park Carla mentioned appeared. It was reassuring to see the area had been cordoned off properly and that the forensics team was already at the scene, along with Lorraine who was in the process of pulling on her white paper suit. She glanced their way and waved as Sara drew the car to a halt alongside Lorraine's van.

"Hi, we meet again." Sara smiled and locked the vehicle after she and Carla climbed out.

"All too soon for my liking. You might want to grab a suit before we set off."

"Is the crime scene very far?" Sara stared ahead at the slight incline that eventually led into the forest.

"Not too far, thank God. You ever been to the top?"

"I have," Carla replied. "Almost killed me when I was younger."

Lorraine laughed. "It's not that bad. Bad enough, though, I suppose."

"I was an unfit teenager at the time, used to sitting in front of the TV playing video games."

"Well, in that case, I can totally understand your comment. Anyway, it's not far. If you're ready, ladies, let's go. I'd leave your paper shoes off until we get closer."

The three of them set off, their blue shoes in hand, ready to slip on once they arrived at the scene. They were all slightly puffed by the time they reached the small clearing. Scattered in front of them within a four-foot radius were five black bags.

"She's in them," Lorraine explained.

"Don't tell me she's been cut up," Sara said, her stomach lurching a little.

Lorraine nodded. "Afraid so. Someone was keen on being thorough."

Carla sighed. "Not that thorough if they decided to dump the body here."

"Hmm...or was their intention for the body to be found?" Sara said, glancing at the scene with trepidation hurtling through her. "Do you have anything at all yet, Lorraine?"

"We know the victim is an Asian woman."

"Okay, that's a start at least. Any ID found? I'm wondering if she's local."

"Nothing so far. I've only had a peep in a couple of the bags." Lorraine stepped forward, opened one of the black bags and invited Sara to take a look.

"Do I have to?"

Lorraine rattled the bag, encouraging her to step forward. Peering into its depths, Sara gasped when the head of a woman gazed up at her. At least, she thought it was a woman. Her face was staved in. Sara was immediately aware that without any form of ID present it was going to be a nigh on impossible task identifying the victim. "Are we talking anthropologist job here?"

"I think so, unless you can match her with a missing person on your records. I'll get an anthropologist working on it as soon as I've finished the PM."

"Excellent news. We'll check with miss pers when we get back; you never know your luck. Do all the sacks contain her remains?"

"Let's see, shall we?" Lorraine undid the other bags which had been knotted a few times. She called out the contents as she went. "Two arms in this one." Moving on to the next bag, she glanced up and announced, "A naked torso in this one."

"Maybe she'll have a distinctive tattoo that will help ID her."

Lorraine turned the torso over and shook her head. "Nothing from what I can see so far. I don't want to disturb her much here. I'd like to take all the bags back to the lab, get any DNA off the sacks, if there is any, that is."

"Good idea. What's in that one?" Sara pointed to the farthest bag.

Lorraine shuffled through the leaves on the ground and, reaching for the bag, pulled it towards her and gasped. "Hang on, what's this?"

Sara and Carla took a few steps closer and leant forward to have a gander. "What?" Sara asked.

Lorraine ignored the sack for a moment and crouched. "I think it's her ID."

"Excellent news, that'll save us a job." Sara's excitement rapidly shot up a few levels.

Lorraine took her time opening the wallet with her gloved hands. She extracted a small card with a photo on it and looked up at Sara with a frown pulling at her brow. "Come closer. I think you'll want to see this."

Sara inched forward and squatted next to Lorraine who angled the card her way. Sara tutted.

"Bloody hell, you two. Talk about keeping a girl in suspense. What is it?" Carla asked, frustration evident in her tone.

"The ID doesn't belong to her. It belongs to the girl we found in the hotel yesterday."

"What?" Carla screeched.

"You heard me. That can only mean one thing: the killer has struck again." Sara stood and shook out the numbness affecting her legs.

"It can also mean that the victims are connected, which should make it easier to identify this girl," Carla pointed out.

"True." Sara blew out a breath. "It also means there could be yet another victim out there."

Carla tilted her head. "How do you come to that conclusion?"

Sara scratched the side of her face with her gloved hand. "Think about it. We've got yet another victim who is missing her ID. My bet is that her ID shows up with another victim, just like we've stumbled across here."

"Crap, I hope you're wrong about that."

"Me, too. Anything else for us, Lorraine? We're going to have to shoot off and see if we can trace the first victim's family. They must be going out of their minds with worry."

"You go. I'll give you a shout if I find anything else," Lorraine said, rising to her feet.

A male member of the forensic team snapped photos of the area once Carla and Sara had moved away from the bags.

"Be in touch soon. Bye for now." Sara waved at Lorraine and set off back down the hill towards the car. "Get on to the station. See if Christine can locate the hotel victim's family for us."

"Doing it now," Carla said. Withdrawing her phone from her pocket, she picked her course carefully, avoiding the odd fallen branch or large tree root emerging through the path as they walked back down the hill. "Christine, can you run the name Lisa Taylor through the system for me? Her address is forty-five Greenly Road, Breinton. Thanks. I'll hang on."

They had disrobed and were seated back in the car before Christine found the information they needed.

"I have her parents down as living at the same address. Do you need anything else? I can find a phone number for you."

"No. We're not far from there now. We'll call round and see if they're in. Thanks, Christine. We'll be back soon." Carla ended the call.

Sara eased her way back down the lane, and Carla gave her directions where to go next as she had a family member who lived in the Breinton area. They pulled up outside the small bungalow a few moments later. There was a silver Mondeo sitting on the drive.

"Looks like someone's home. Damn, I hate this part. Come on, let's get it over with."

They left the car and walked up the narrow path. Either side of them, daffodils were coming into bloom.

"Spring has officially sprung when these guys show their true colours," Carla pointed out.

Sara smiled and rang the bell, her smile dropping as soon as she heard the chain being fiddled with on the other side of the door.

A grey-haired woman in her early sixties greeted them warmly. "Hello there, how can I help?"

"If it's that damned double-glazing salesman again, tell him I'll ring the police if he doesn't stop harassing us. No means bloody no," a man's angry voice travelled through the house.

The woman rolled her eyes. "Can you tell he hates salesmen knocking on the door? I hope you're not in that line of business, dears."

"We're not." Sara flashed her ID in the woman's face. "I'm DI Sara Ramsey, and this is my partner, DS Carla Jameson. Are you Mrs Taylor?"

"I am. May I ask why you're here? It's Flora, by the way."

"Would it be possible to come in and speak with you and your husband for a few minutes? It is important."

"Of course. Oh dear, now you've got my mind racing. Thinking about what laws we've broken. I can't think of anything offhand."

Sara smiled and placed a reassuring hand on the woman's arm. "You haven't done anything wrong, I assure you."

"Phew, that's good to know."

She closed the front door behind them and led them through to the back of the house to a large conservatory where a gentleman of around the same age was sitting in one of the wicker armchairs, reading a newspaper. He stood as soon as Sara and Carla entered the room.

"Gerald, these ladies are with the local police. They want to see us both."

"Police, you say? What are the police doing knocking at my door? We've not done anything wrong, not that I know of anyway."

"Hello, Mr Taylor. Please, why don't you both take a seat? You're right, you've done nothing wrong."

Mrs Taylor dropped into the armchair next to her husband's and he retook his seat, a worried expression written on both of their faces as they reached for each other's hands.

"May we sit?" Sara asked.

The pair nodded.

Sara sat on the edge of the sofa, apprehension coursing through her veins. "Mr and Mrs Taylor, do you have a daughter by the name of Lisa?"

"We do. Why? What's she done?" Mr Taylor asked aggressively.

"Hush, now, Gerald. Let the police officer speak. Go on, what about Lisa?"

"Have you heard from her lately?"

"Not for a few days. She's away on a business course—at least, that's what she told us. Is she in some kind of trouble?" Mrs Taylor asked anxiously.

"Do you know where the course is being held?"

The couple looked at each other and shrugged. "We don't. Our daughter is very secretive at the best of times. In the Midlands somewhere."

"What type of course is it? What career does she have?"

"Not sure what type of course. She works for a dentist, though, as a dental nurse," Mrs Taylor said.

"For a local dentist?"

"Yes, I can get you their details if you want." Mrs Taylor left the room and came back with a card for Foster's Dental Surgery in Hereford.

Sara took the card. "Thank you. May I keep this?"

"Of course. Please, can you tell me what this is all about? You're worrying me."

"Sit down, Mrs Taylor."

The woman sat and clutched her husband's hand once again.

"Yesterday we were called to a hotel in the city centre where an unidentified female's body was found in one of the rooms. We believe the body to be that of your daughter, Lisa."

"What? That's impossible. You said the body was unidentified. This doesn't make sense," Mr Taylor shot back quickly while Mrs Taylor broke down in tears. "Hush now, Flora. Let me hear what the officer has to say."

"Sorry, all day yesterday we tried to identify your daughter, even putting an image of her booking into the hotel on the news last night. Today, we were called to another murder scene, and alongside the victim's body we found your daughter's ID, which led us here to you today."

"Murder? You said murder. Are you telling us that someone took our daughter's life?" Mr Taylor demanded. He slung an arm around his wife's trembling shoulders.

"Sorry, but yes. Do you have any idea why your daughter would book into a hotel under an assumed name? That's why we had trouble identifying her yesterday."

They both shook their heads, then Mr Taylor said, "Not a clue. And the hotel was in Hereford, you say?"

"That's right."

"Why? Why would she stay in a hotel in the same city she lives in? None of this makes any sense." Mr Taylor ran a hand through his short grey hair.

"That's what we need to find out. Do you know what the course was about?"

The couple glanced at each other and shrugged. "No, she didn't say. It was work related, and she rarely discusses her work with us," Mrs Taylor replied.

"Don't worry, we'll call by her place of work after we've left here. Maybe they'll be able to fill in some of the gaps for us. Tell me, was your daughter married?"

"No."

"Was she in a relationship?"

"She went out occasionally. Although our daughter lived with us, she lived her own life. We didn't pry into each other's business at all," Mr Taylor told her.

"I see. So she didn't bring anyone back here, introduce you to anyone she was seeing?"

The couple shook their heads again.

"What about friends? Maybe they'll be able to help us."

"She used to be friendly with a girl called Mandy. She told us she worked with her at the dental surgery. Maybe she'll be able to answer your questions. I'm sorry we're so useless at all this. I suppose we're in shock." Mrs Taylor rested her head on her husband's shoulder.

He squeezed her tightly and glanced at Sara. "Please find whoever did this to our daughter. We won't be able to rest until we know this person has been caught. No parent should have to suffer like this, knowing that their child has been murdered."

"Please, I want to assure you, we won't rest until we've caught the killer. I think we've covered everything now. One last thing, we'll need to check your daughter's possessions."

"Of course. Now?"

"I'll make the necessary arrangements and get someone to call you. Are you going to be all right? I can get a family liaison officer to come and sit with you if you prefer."

"We'll be fine, in time." Mr Taylor rose from his chair and left the room.

"Sorry for your loss, Mrs Taylor. Hopefully we'll be in touch again soon." Sara held her hand out for the woman to shake and then left the room ahead of Carla.

Mr Taylor was in the hallway holding the front door open. Sara held her hand out.

He shook it briefly and lowered his voice so his wife couldn't hear. "You have my permission to punish the bastard who did this in his cell, if you get my drift?"

"I do, sir. That won't be happening. You'll just have to accept my assurance that the murderer will be dealt with in the appropriate way. Take care of your wife."

"I will, don't worry."

They stepped over the threshold, and the draught from the door closing swiftly behind them crawled up Sara's back. Sara exhaled a breath and they walked back to the car. "That was tough. I can understand the father's reaction. It hits you hard when someone you love gets kill…" Her voice drifted off as she contemplated her own situation, unsure what the heck was going on with Mark. By the screams she'd heard the previous night, it would suggest the gang was intent on punishing him if only for her benefit. She was none the wiser about what was happening. The gang hadn't requested anything from her as yet; they were toying with her.

They reached the car and got in. "Hey, where did you drift off to?"

Sara shook the vile images of Mark being trussed up somewhere, waiting for his next torture session, from her mind. "Sorry, just thinking about what our next step should be."

"We need to go to the dental surgery, don't we?"

"Of course. I meant after that. What if her boss or this Mandy can't enlighten us about anything, then what?"

Carla twisted in her seat to look at her. "This isn't like you, boss. To think negatively. What's eating you?"

"Certain cases you get a feeling about. I guess this is one of those cases."

"A doomed feeling? So early on in the investigation?"

Sara shrugged and started the engine. "Talking bollocks as usual, I know. Let's see what her work colleagues have to say about Lisa, shall we?"

CHAPTER 6

AFTER WEAVING their way through the heavy traffic, they parked in the dentist car park and entered the tall building. The receptionist offered them a pearly white smile. "Hi, do you have an appointment?"

Sara flashed her ID. "We'd like to see the person in charge, if they're available."

"Oh! May I give them a clue what it's about?"

"We'd rather tell them that." Sara peered at the young woman's name badge. Mandy. Was she the Mandy who was Lisa's best friend?

Her smile still fixed in place, Mandy left the desk and returned a few seconds later with a tall man in his forties. He wore a pale-blue overshirt and white trousers. "Hi, I'm Michael Ward, the head dentist here. Actually, I own the place. How may I help?"

"Is there somewhere more private where we can chat, sir?"

"I'm with a patient at present. Can this wait?"

"How long are you likely to be?"

His head tilted from side to side. "About ten minutes, give or take. I have a free appointment slot after that if you're willing to wait."

"We'll sit here until you're ready, sir."

Mr Ward frowned, nodded and rushed back to his patient.

"Can I get you ladies a drink while you're waiting?"

"A coffee would be nice, thank you, Mandy."

"I'll have the same," Carla chipped in.

Once they were alone, Carla asked, "You think that's Lisa's friend, don't you?"

"Don't you?"

Mandy returned with two mugs of coffee on a small tray and a sugar bowl. "I should have asked if you took sugar. Ignore the lumps. You know what men are like. They tend to stick their spoon in the coffee and then in the sugar. We're constantly fishing the lumps out."

"Thanks, not to worry. We'll sort it. Are you busy, Mandy?"

"Busy filing and keeping the appointments up to date, nothing that can't wait. Why?"

Sara gestured for the young woman to take a seat. "I wondered if you're the same Mandy who is best friends with Lisa Taylor."

"That's right. Why do you ask?"

"That's why we're here today. We're trying to find out more about Lisa. Do you think you can help us?"

Mandy shuffled forward in her chair. "I'll try. She's away on holiday at the moment. Has she done something wrong?"

"Not that we know of. Where is she?"

Mandy twisted her lips as she thought. "Crikey, I should know. I think she said she was going back to Portugal. I might be wrong, though. When you asked if we are best friends, that might be stretching the truth a little."

"Oh, care to clarify that statement?"

"We fell out a month or so ago. Over something so trivial I can't even remember what it was about. I overheard her talking to one of the other dental nurses, Janine, that's how I know she's gone away."

"That's a shame. Were you friends for long?"

"Yes, years. We went everywhere together. Were always staying over at each other's house, up until last year." Mandy's chin dropped.

"Please try and think back to what went wrong between you."

"I'm trying. Okay, it was over a fella. I said I fancied this fella at the Classy Jive nightclub, and she was the one who copped off with him. I was furious with her. It's not the done thing to do that to a mate, is it?"

"Can't say I've ever been in such a position, but no, I agree with you, I don't think it's the done thing between friends. Do you know what happened with this fella? I mean, was it a one-night stand or did it blossom into a relationship perhaps?"

"I really couldn't tell you. I lost interest after they left the nightclub together that evening."

"Sorry to hear that. Can you recall the date when the incident happened?"

"Around Christmas time, that's why I was so pissed off with her."

"Maybe this Janine would be able to fill in the gaps for us. Is she at work today?"

"She is. Not sure if she can or not. You'll have to ask her. Can you tell me what Lisa has done wrong? That fella wasn't dodgy, was he?"

"We can't, not at this moment in time. We're simply conducting enquiries after some information has come our way," Sara replied vaguely.

"I see. Sorry I asked. Ever the nosy parker, that's me."

"Perhaps you can tell me when Lisa was due back. To work, I mean."

"She's on the shift manifest for next week. It was pinned on the noticeboard only yesterday. All right if I get back to work now? The boss is a bit of an ogre if things aren't completed on time."

"Of course. Thanks for chatting with us."

Mandy left her seat and returned to the reception area to continue with her duties. Sara and Carla sat in silence as they drank their coffees until Michael Ward reappeared. He left the patient with Mandy to deal with and requested that Sara and Carla join him in his treatment room.

"Sorry to keep you waiting. Now, what can I do for you?"

Sara produced her ID. "Thank you for giving us a moment of your time, Mr Ward. We appreciate how busy you must be. I'm DI Sara Ramsey, and this is DS Carla Jameson. We're here today to ask a few questions about one of your employees, if that's okay?"

His brow furrowed. "Which one? We employ ten staff here."

"Lisa Taylor."

"Lisa? She's on holiday right now. Don't tell me she's been up to no good and banged up in a cell somewhere abroad?"

"No. She hasn't. I'd like to know more about her before I reveal the real reason behind our visit, sir. We've had a chat with Mandy, who used to be her best friend, I believe."

"I think so. What's going on?"

"The thing is, we visited her parents earlier on, and Lisa told them that she was on a course, a business course."

"What? Why would she lie like that?"

"This is what we intend to find out. We'd like to know if Lisa ever revealed to either you or the other members of your staff whether she was in any kind of trouble."

"Trouble? What sort of trouble?"

Sara blew out a frustrated breath. "We're at a loss to know that, sir." She was desperately trying not to reveal that Lisa had been murdered but found it a strain what with the questions going round and round and not getting anywhere. "Mandy hinted at a possible connection with a man that caused a rift between them. Did you hear about that incident?"

"No. I tend to steer clear of any problems between the staff unless it affects the way they carry out their jobs. Unless you're asking me about something specific, Inspector, then I'm afraid I can't help you."

"That's a shame. Maybe you'll allow us to question the other members of staff while we're here."

"Feel free. Providing your interviews don't get in the way of the practice running smoothly."

"We'll do our best."

I can show you to the canteen and ask the staff to come and see you one by one when they're free, if that'll help?"

"That would be amazing. Thank you."

They followed Mr Ward out of the treatment room and along a narrow corridor to a rest area at the back of the property which contained a small kitchen and four chairs and a table shoved up against one of the walls.

"Not the most glamorous of settings, granted."

"Don't worry. It's on a par with what we used to have down at the station until they closed it due to insufficient funds. Would it be possible to speak to Janine first?"

"Of course. I'll go and see if she's free and send her through. Good luck."

The next hour consisted of asking the same questions over and over again to all the staff at the surgery, and in that time, it was only Janine who could tell them anything. Even then, her answers had been relatively vague and not what they wanted to hear.

She'd told them that Lisa had started going out with the man she'd met at the nightclub but refused to tell anyone his name. Once Sara heard that, her heart seemed to sink into her stomach. He was the one missing link she was eager to get hold of to question.

Once all the interviews had taken place, Sara and Carla walked back to the reception area. Michael Ward was there chatting with a patient. They waited a few moments for him to finish and for the patient to leave.

Sara extended her hand for him to shake. "Thank you for allowing us to interview your staff. I didn't want to mention this before because I didn't want to jeopardise any information coming our way. It is with regret that I have to tell you that Lisa Taylor was found murdered yesterday at a hotel in Hereford."

Both Michael's and Mandy's mouths gaped open.

Eventually, once the fact had sunk in, Michael recovered enough to say, "Jesus, really? Now I get why you're here. I hope the staff have been helpful to you. Bloody hell! Murdered? Sorry, it's only just dawning on me what you said. Who would do such a thing? She was a decent enough girl from what I could tell."

"That's what we intend to find out, sir. Sorry to have to break the news to you in this way." Sara glanced at the receptionist who staggered a little. "Mandy, are you okay?"

"I don't know," Mandy replied quietly before she fainted.

"Shit! Mandy, are you all right?" Michael rushed behind the desk, and Sara followed.

"Let me get to her." Michael stepped aside. "Mandy? Mandy, can you hear me?"

Sara felt for a pulse. It was slower than the normal rate. "Carla, nip and fetch a glass of water, please?"

Carla rushed back to the staff restroom and returned with a glass of water. Sara tapped Mandy on the cheek and continued to call her name until finally the young woman's eyes flickered open.

"What happened?" Mandy asked, her voice croaky.

Sara held the glass up to her lips. "Here, drink this. You passed out. No damage done."

Mandy sipped at the water, and her face screwed up. "Ugh…I hate water. I'm so sorry, I don't know what came over me. Is she really dead?"

"I'm afraid so. Can you stand up?"

Mandy leant on Sara for support as she tried to stand. Her legs almost gave way beneath her again, but Sara clung to her arm to prevent her from falling. "Oh dear. My legs feel like jelly, can I sit down?"

Michael wheeled the receptionist's chair alongside Sara and Mandy and took hold of Mandy's other arm to help lower the young woman into the chair.

"Thank you. I feel such a fool. I don't think I've ever fainted in my life before. It came as such a shock. I thought you were here because Lisa was in some kind of trouble."

"Don't worry. It happens a lot at times such as this. Are you sure you're going to be all right?" Sara said.

Mandy nodded. "I'm feeling much better now, a little light-headed."

"Don't worry, we'll take good care of Mandy," Michael stated with a smile aimed at his receptionist.

Sara nodded. "If you're sure. Okay, we'd better be on our way then. I'm so sorry we had to break the news to you. I take it neither of you watched the local news last night?"

They both shrugged and shook their heads.

"We ran Lisa's photo on the bulletin. At the time, we didn't know her identity. That came to light today at a different location."

"I hope you find the person who did this to Lisa soon," Michael said. "I imagine her parents must be devastated."

"They are. Once again, thank you for allowing us to question the staff. I hope the news doesn't come as too much of a shock to the others. I'll leave you my card. If anyone thinks of anything that you believe would help our investigation, please ring me, day or night."

Michael picked up the card off the desk and placed it somewhere behind the counter. "We will. I promise you."

Sara and Carla left the building. Outside, Sara stood against the wall as the fresh air took the wind out of her sails.

"Hey, are you okay?"

Sara smiled weakly at her partner. "I'm fine. Just give me a second to recover. Thank God Mandy was all right and we didn't have to call an ambulance."

"Horrendous when that happens. There's no telling if they've fainted or if their heart has given out on them through shock."

"Exactly. God, what I wouldn't give for a large brandy right now."

"We could have a sneaky one across the road. I won't tell if you won't."

"Knowing our luck, the DCI will walk in and catch us. Tell you what we'll do. Grab an OJ and a sandwich instead, my treat."

"You don't have to do that. I can pay my own way."

"I know you can. I'm feeling generous."

"Okay, you've twisted my arm."

They walked across the busy road to the White Swan and ordered their food and drinks from the barmaid, then took a seat tucked away in the corner.

"So, what do we have?" Sara asked, taking a sip from her drink.

Carla shrugged. "We've got a possible boyfriend angle that we need to look into, even though it's a bit vague."

Sara glanced around the pub, which was beginning to fill up fast as it was now almost one o'clock. "Too vague for my liking. We're going to need to get on to the nightclub, trawl through their CCTV discs and see if we can at least get an image of this guy. I know we've got a sighting at the hotel, but in truth, we don't know if that person's connected to Lisa yet or not."

"That's true. Where do we go from here?"

"We'll have lunch then go back to the station. Action the CCTV discs from the nightclub and the surrounding area to try and catch either of them on the footage. Without identifying that man, then we're like ducks in croc-infested waters."

Carla chuckled. "You do come out with the weirdest things. All right, there's one other thing we haven't had time to cover yet."

"I know what you're getting at: the body in the bags. There has to be a connection because of Lisa Taylor's ID being found at the scene, but what? It's going to take a while before we get anything from the forensic team. Anthropologists can take several weeks to deliver a model we can work with."

"That's not ideal, but what else can we do? I know we rely on CCTV footage a lot, but there's nothing out there at Credenhill, possibly why the killer chose to leave the bags there."

The waitress appeared with their thick doorstep sandwiches. "Thanks."

"Do you need anything else?"

"Not at the moment," Sara replied.

"Enjoy your lunch," the waitress said then left.

Sara lifted up the edge of her sandwich to see the amount of filling inside. "Jesus, must be a whole tin of tuna squished in there. I'm never going to eat all that."

Carla laughed. "Glad I chose a cheese and pickle one, although the size of the wedge of cheese I have, I don't think I'll be eating anything else today. At least you can ask for a 'cat bag' and take the remains home for Misty."

Sara screwed up her face. "If it was straight tuna and not smothered in mayonnaise, I think she'd lap it up. Anyway, back to what we were saying before. I agree that's probably why the killer chose the woodland location, which is infuriating at best for us. Again, our hands are tied until we can name the victim. Seems to me we have a killer who is intent on messing with us. Why else would he leave Lisa Taylor's ID with the second victim? I can't stand arseholes who think they're better than us. Makes me even more determined to bring the bastard down." There was more venom in her words than she'd planned because of her own situation. She was tempted to tell Carla, but the warning from the kidnappers put paid to that.

Please, don't hurt Mark any more than you have done already.

"Hey, there you go again, drifting off and ignoring my response."

"Sorry. You know my mind has a life of its own at times. It's a struggle to keep it in line most days."

"You're forgiven. Andrew rang last night. I wasn't sure if I should tell you or not."

"I would never judge you. What did he have to say for himself?"

"He grovelled. Said how sorry he was and that he missed me. Also asked if he could drop by over the weekend and take me out for dinner."

"Wow, the bloody cheek of him. What did you say?" Sara could tell that Carla was contemplating the proposal. "Look, far be it for me to tell you to stay clear of the creep, and yes, I did say the word *creep*. He deserves that tag after the way he treated you. Take a step back and really consider what he put you through. If any man cheated on me, he'd have his dick chopped off—yes, I'm that serious. Men should have the guts to finish with a woman first before they make the decision to go after another one. Sorry, I went off on one there. This type of thing riles me. Most men want to have their cake and eat it."

"Crikey! I wish I hadn't mentioned it now. You didn't even give me a chance to respond. For your information, I told him to stick his offer up his arse. I know I'm still hurting and lonely at times, but going back is never the answer. My mum drummed that into me years ago. If I'm honest with you, I found myself cringing all the time he was on the phone with me."

Sara laughed. "Why the heck didn't you just hang up on the prick?"

"I was intrigued to hear what he had to say. He was grovelling. It's always good to hear a bloke do that."

"I suppose so. Christ, if any man ever did that to me, I'd make sure

THE DEAD CAN'T SPEAK

he got the hint never to try and contact me in the future." She reached across the table. "You'll find someone worthy of your affections soon. I know you will."

"Like you did with Mark?"

Sara's gaze dropped down to the half-eaten sandwich she'd nibbled at. "Don't judge me. I called it quits with him to try and save him. Who knows what lies ahead of me in the imminent future?" *I know all right, and I'm scared, not only of what the future has in store for me but of revealing the truth to my partner. Shit! Why does life have to be this hard?*

"Hello, anybody in there? You drifted off again. It's a good job I'm not the type who gets offended easily."

"Sorry. I guess my head is all over the place, what with breaking up with Mark and dealing with a complex case. You have my word from now on that I'll only be concentrating on the case or cases in the foreseeable future."

"You're nuts. It's crazy of you to ditch Mark when it's obvious you're head over heels in love with the guy."

Tears misted Sara's eyes, and she pushed her plate to the middle of the table. "It's for the best."

"Best for who? I bet both of you are bloody miserable. Christ, Sara, isn't life short enough as it is? Grab the happiness while it's there. Okay, enough lectures from me. I don't have the right to give out relationship advice after my latest one ended in disaster."

"I know you mean well. I have my reasons for not pursuing things with Mark. Can we agree to differ on the topic?"

"Okay, if you insist. But you should seriously consider getting back with him."

Sara tilted her head.

Carla continued, "Have you any idea what the statistics are for coppers finding the love of their lives? Well, I don't know what they actually are either, but I bet they're not good. All I'm saying is, that if you're happy with Mark, let things ride between you. You can always opt out if things start going down the pan in a few months."

Sara held her hands up. "Which is what I've done. Ended it before it gets too serious and one of us gets hurt. At the end of the day, I have to realise I'll never have the kind of fulfilling relationship I had with Philip. I just decided that second-best wasn't good enough. End of subject. Drink up, we'd better get back to work. We have a possible serial killer on our hands."

"You know what, boss, sometimes, I could slap you for being you. True happiness comes around once in a lifetime, twice to certain people if they're extremely lucky. I believe you're one of those people. I saw the way that dishy Mark looked at you and the depth of his kiss outside the station a few weeks ago."

Sara downed the rest of her orange juice and left the table without uttering another word. She couldn't, there was a lump in her throat the size of a football. Carla caught up with her when she was three feet from the car.

"I'm sorry. I didn't mean to push you like that."

"You didn't. Let's just say there are things you don't know and leave it at that for now, Carla." She smiled across the roof of the car and then slid behind the steering wheel.

After buckling up, Carla said, "I'm always here if you need to chat."

"I know. Ditto, matey. Let's make a pact to put our personal problems aside during our working day, deal?"

They shook hands. "For now. Can we revisit it when either one of us gets another fella, though?"

"We'll reconsider, should the situation differ in the near future."

CHAPTER 7

"Hi, it's me. How are you fixed for tonight?" he asked, his voice light and enticing.

"Well, it depends what you're offering."

He smiled. The hook had been yanked; she was up for meeting him. He liked Jemima. She had sexy curves and a body he loved to devour. She'd never let him down, not like some of the others. She was always willing to spread her legs for him and the other men he sent her way.

"Okay, you know I'll treat you like a goddess. You mean the world to me, Jemima."

"I know you will. Where and when?"

"Eight o'clock at the Happy Hound pub. I'll book us a room in a swanky hotel. Spoil you a little. How does that sound?"

"Wonderful. I'll make sure I spend the rest of the day making myself beautiful for you. See you later."

He hung up and rubbed his hands together. He knew he was taking a risk, still being in Hereford, but the police had nothing on him yet. If they had, he'd be all over the news by now. All they'd put out so far was the image from the hotel of 'someone wearing a hat'.

That shot could have been of dozens, if not thousands of men, instead of him.

Luckily, he knew the city well. There were intimate hotels aplenty to choose from, and the same went for places where he could dispose of the bodies, too.

He stared at his reflection and wondered if Jemima would appreciate his disguise. His colour was normally black, but he'd dyed his hair blond. He turned sideways, admiring the new shade and the difference it had made to his whole appearance. It made him wonder how many other killers went to this much trouble to evade capture. He'd figured out long ago that it was his life's ambition to fool around with the police. It had taken him years to build up to this stage. To get all the girls on board. Now that he'd accomplished that, it was time to kill them one by one.

In readiness for his hot date that evening, he showered and spent the next few hours preening himself to perfection. If women could take an eternity to achieve the right look, then so could he. Staring into his wardrobe at the many suits displayed on the silver rail, he withdrew them one at a time. An image of the last time he'd worn each of the suits flicked through his mind. He laughed at some of the images and felt sad at others. It was the happier moments that lingered the longest. The moments when he'd ended someone's life. There were bodies scattered the length and breadth of the UK, fifty at the last count. Disposing of the women and not leaving any DNA behind was the easy part, but he needed something more. To up his game. He was eager to experience the rush of adrenaline speeding through his veins.

Leaving the ID of the previous victim with the next corpse had given him a thrill that he'd never felt before in his life. He glanced down at the erection straining against his zip. He punched the air in elation but resisted the temptation to shout, not wishing to bring attention to himself from the neighbours. He hadn't lived in his house for long. It was good to finally have a base where he could come home and relax, although he never, ever brought the women here.

No, he always gave them the impression that he lived an executive lifestyle in a penthouse suite based in a city hotel. The fools believed him, too. Why? Because of the expensive suits he'd invested in. The same suits he was contemplating right now. His father had always instilled in him that clothes maketh the man. That was the only thing his father ever did for him. Most of the time he'd thrashed the living daylights out of him just for being in the same room as him. His mother had walked out on them a few years earlier—at least that was what his father had told him. After that day, in order to survive, he'd mostly lived on his wits, sourcing food where he could as his father never shopped or kept food in the house. He ate out all the time, just him. He'd decided enough was enough and had left his family home at the ripe old age of twelve. He'd lived a punishing life on the streets until an old lady had taken him under her wing. Steering him in the right direction, she'd helped him to make the right kind of contacts to survive being homeless for the next three years.

Eventually, at the age of fifteen, he'd worked in restaurants, living on the premises, in the stockrooms, piled high with rotting veg and listening to the sound of the rats scurrying past him in the dark. He hadn't been scared; his vivid imagination had been his saviour come the end.

He'd achieved his lucky break when one of the owners of the new restaurant where he was working had taken a shine to him. Mai Ling had pitied him, given him a place to stay and supplied clothes for him. Once he'd smartened himself up, she'd promoted him to the role of assistant manager. He'd never looked back, refusing to dwell on his loveless past. She was also kind enough to let him into her bed. He'd learnt how to satisfy a woman and the measures needed to keep her content.

He'd taken to the extracurricular training, and within months, Mai Ling had promoted him to manager. He'd revelled in the power he had over the staff, who had once laughed at him. It had built his self-esteem and moulded his character.

Mai Ling had been proud of him in so many ways. She'd been getting older and had decided to alter her will. She'd sat him down one day and informed him that she was leaving her entire estate to him. Her restaurant, her home, everything. He'd hugged her and showed his gratitude in bed that night.

As soon as the paperwork had been confirmed and she'd shown him the documents, he'd conjured up a plan to kill the old woman. It had always been his ambition to leave China and travel to the UK. With a lot of money lining his pockets, he could fulfil that ambition.

He had hired a few homeless people, given them more money than they'd ever held in their hands and instructed them to buy some balaclavas. Then he'd told them to storm the restaurant just before closing time. He'd even told one of the men to strike him to make it look like an authentic robbery.

They had successfully killed Mai Ling and hurt the other members of staff still on duty, then ran off with the night's takings.

He'd met up with the gang in the early hours of the morning to reclaim the restaurant's takings. At first the men were reluctant to hand over the money. In the end, he'd had to forge another deal with them. Instead of walking away with all the cash, he'd relinquished fifty percent. It was enough to stash away and would cover his fare to the UK.

The settlement of the will had taken longer than he'd anticipated—six weeks in total. Money had been tight in those six weeks, but after the will had been read, he was a very rich man, in Chinese terms. Although once he'd arrived in the UK, he'd found his money hadn't stretched very far at all. So he'd hatched another plan, had seen an opening in a tried-and-tested market and pounced on the idea. All that was three years ago. In that time, the money had rolled in, thanks to the women he had taken under *his* wing.

Now he wanted more from life and was eager to obtain it quickly. But first he had a lot of cleaning up to do.

He walked into the Happy Hound pub with ten minutes to spare. He glanced around the interior, searching for his date. He should have known better than to expect Jemima to be sitting there waiting for him. She was always late, something that wound him up tighter than a coiled spring. He exhaled a large breath to calm himself. *It's still early, give her time.*

Five minutes after eight, the leggy blonde entered the public bar, swaying her curvaceous hips towards him, fully aware of the impact she was having on all the customers in the public bar. He proudly glanced around to see the women glaring at her and the men openly admiring her beauty. It tore at his heart to think of what was to come later. But he was on a mission. It was imperative for him to stick to his agenda.

He stood to greet her, kissed her on both cheeks and pulled out the chair facing him. Once she was seated, he placed his hands on her shoulders and massaged her neck a little, aware of how much Jemima loved the feel of his hands on her, especially in that area. He smiled as an image of what he was going to do to her in a few hours back at the hotel surfaced in his mind.

"How are you? Your hair suits you in that colour," she said. Her long, thin, prettily manicured fingers covered his hand when he retook his seat.

"Couldn't be better. I'm thrilled you decided to come on a date with me this evening. It's been a while since we enjoyed each other's company."

"It has. Too long. We've both been so busy lately, earning money," she added. A twinkle appeared in her eye at the mention of money.

"We have. It's so nice to have some downtime and to be spending that time with my favourite girl."

"Get on with you. I bet you say that to all your girls."

She was right. He did. But it didn't stop him enjoying her company more than the others'. She was easier to manipulate. He'd done things with her that he never knew existed in this life. She was an expert in her field at pleasing men. She'd been doing it for ten years or more and it had now become second nature to her. Most men treated her like a goddess. He had more compliments from the punters about Jemima than all the other girls put together.

He chuckled and let out a satisfied sigh. It would be difficult to say goodbye to Jemima, but it was time to move on, to grander and newer pastures far away from here. He was determined not to think of her fate; he wanted to spend the next few hours charming his date.

Treating her like a queen. She had been his top earner over the years. This was his way of paying her back for all the loyalty she'd shown him, to spend some of *his* precious time with her.

He ordered a bottle of prosecco with their meal of steak and chips.

"Gosh, there's a lot here," Jemima commented when the waitress placed their meals in front of them. "Not sure I'll eat all the chips. You know what they say, a moment on the lips is a lifetime on the hips."

He leant across the table and whispered seductively, "I'm sure we'll think of a way to work off the calories later, lovely. Fill your boots."

Her cheeks coloured up under his intense gaze. "Okay, if you insist. We could be looking at an all-nighter, just warning you."

He raised his eyebrows. "Sounds an ideal solution to the problem. Bring it on. Now, eat up. I noticed they had salted caramel cheesecake on the menu. Sounds tempting, doesn't it?"

She raised her eyebrows and whispered sexily, "Umm...delicious. I'd rather be wearing it than eating it, though."

He almost choked on the mouthful of steak he was chewing on.

She laughed raucously, drawing admiring glances from the crowd. That was when it hit him. *Shit! We're drawing attention to ourselves. Not ideal for what I have planned.*

He smiled at her and concentrated on his food until his plate was empty. By the time he'd finished, the waistband on his trousers was cutting into his midriff. Defeated, he said, "Sod the pudding, I don't think I have room for anything else. Do you?"

"I have room for something, and it's not food." She chortled.

Her red-painted lips parted to reveal her perfectly formed white teeth—one of the attributes that had attracted him to her in the first place. Her smile was a magnet, tempting him. She'd developed well under his guidance over the years. Learnt to make more of her sultry looks and stunning figure.

It was a shame all that was going to go to waste later.

They spent the next half an hour touching each other's hands and laughing. Guilt clawed at his chest every time her smile beamed.

"Are you ready?"

One of her eyebrows lifted into her blonde fringe. "For what?"

He left his seat and held his arm out for her to take. She slipped hers through his and walked out of the pub towards his car.

For the briefest of moments, he pondered whether he was doing the right thing. He'd had two glasses of wine and was about to get behind the wheel of his vehicle. What if the police pulled him over for drink-driving? *No, they're not likely to do that if I'm careful.*

"Oh dear, I can't seem to walk in a straight line."

"That won't matter when you're lying beneath me."

She giggled and slapped his arm. "You are awful, but I like you."

"How much do you like me? Are you willing to do anything and everything I ask?" he whispered close to her ear before he opened the passenger door.

"Anything and everything, without a doubt," she replied, her speech slightly slurred.

He guided her into her seat and rushed around the car to hop in the driver's seat.

Moments later, he pulled out of the car park and headed to a secluded place he'd recently discovered. He drew the car to a halt in the deserted patch of ground where some people parked their cars. Not tonight, though.

She turned to him, looking surprised. "What are we doing here?"

"I thought it would be fun. You know, doing it in the car rather than go back to the hotel. The truth is, I can't wait."

She shrugged her bare shoulders. "Whatever floats your boat, sweetie, you know that. Shall we get in the back?"

"Why not. It's a beautiful spot, isn't it? Shame the weather isn't warmer. We could have made love on the riverbank, listening to the river gently rippling past us."

"I've got a different kind of ebbing and flowing in mind. Come on."

They both got out of the front seats and jumped in the back. Her sexy black dress with all its layers got in the way at first, but he persevered and managed to disrobe her within a few minutes. She laid on the back seat looking sexy as hell as he stripped off his own clothes. He hadn't intended to have sex with her this evening, but the temptation proved to be far too much for him to ignore in the end. He wanted to be inside her for one final time. He attached a condom.

She took over for a while, pleased him like no other woman had ever been able to in the past. Then he was back on top, building to his crescendo. His hands slipped around her throat. To begin with, there was nothing but adulation glinting in her eyes. However, the more he tightened his grip, the more the panic set in. Her long nails tore at his hands, trying to loosen the grip pressing down on her windpipe, but when that didn't work, she stretched up and tried to claw at his face. He had the good sense to pull his head back out of reach. A smile set in place, he squeezed harder as she gasped her final breath.

After all the struggle and life left her body, he bent down and kissed her lips. "Forgive me, my angel. The time has come for you to leave me. I will forever be in your gratitude. Your last supper and fuck were better than anticipated, I'm sure you'll agree."

He spent the next ten minutes getting himself dressed and then struggling to pull her limp body into position so he could dress her once more. With the task completed, he pushed her out of the car, removed a small bag from the glove compartment and tied it around her wrist. Satisfied his next stage of the plan was in place, he dragged her to the water's edge, kissed her one final time and threw her into the River Wye. He watched her body drift for a while before the current took over. He stayed there, riveted to the spot, feeling no remorse.

Returning to the car, he searched the footwell in the back and removed the condom he'd used. He'd get rid of that at home. *Best not to leave any DNA close by for the cops to find.* He laughed and hopped back in his vehicle, feeling accomplished in his mission. Now all he had to do was drive home carefully.

One more down. Only one to go.

CHAPTER 8

AFTER AN UNEVENTFUL AFTERNOON at the station, Sara ordered the team to leave and be back at their desks for eight the following morning.

Carla walked her to the car. "Are you sure you don't want to go for that drink now that we've finished for the day?"

"Would you be disappointed if I said no? I really do want to get home early this evening."

"Any particular reason?" Carla raised her hand in an apology. "Sorry, I shouldn't pry. Promise to ring me if you need me."

Sara rubbed her partner's upper arm. "You worry too much. Take care of yourself first, Carla. Have a good evening."

"You, too. See you bright and early."

Sara waved and slipped into her car. She placed her mobile on the seat beside her and began her journey back home. The traffic was heavy to begin with but became lighter the farther she got away from the city. Her heart thumped the second she spotted Mark's car outside her home. Pulling into her drive, she collected her bag and phone and walked along the path to her house.

"Hey, I was hoping I'd bump into you." Ted's voice startled her.

She spun around, a smile fixed in place. "Hi, Ted. How's it diddling?"

"I haven't heard that in years. My father used to say it all the time when I was a young lad. Fair to middling—how are you? See your fella's been here all day." He pointed his chin at Mark's car.

"Yes, sorry, is it in the way? Mark had to go on a course. I dropped him to the station last night after he got back with the boys. I told him to leave the car here. Should have asked him to leave it on the drive really, never thought it would be an issue."

"Hey, calm down. I didn't say it was a problem. Just making small talk. Is everything all right? You look tired and seem stressed, Sara."

"Tired after a frustrating day at work. A new case landed on my desk a few days ago. They all seem to come with a lot of frustration for us until the pieces start slotting into place. Comes with the territory, I suppose. We'll get there. How's Mavis?"

"She's fine. She told me to come over and ask if you'd like to have supper with us. We'll understand if you say no."

"Oh, Ted, ordinarily I'd love to. The thing is, I'm expecting an important call this evening. It would be better if I was at home when that call finally comes through."

"No problem. It was only cottage pie. Another time, eh? I'll tell her to give you more notice in the future."

She closed the distance between them and kissed him on the cheek. "Pass on my apologies, and thanks for the invitation. Roll on spring, eh? Decent weather and lighter nights. We'll make up for it then, okay?"

"That's a done deal. I'm a dab hand with the barbeque. Dare say that young man of yours is handy with a pair of tongs and charcoal, too. Enjoy your evening, and make sure you don't spend it all on the phone. You need to learn to relax, be like the rest of us, you hear me?"

"Yes, Ted." She gave him a quick kiss again and walked back to the house. Misty was on the other side of the door, as usual. Sara gave her cat an extra-long cuddle then placed her on the floor while she kicked off her shoes and hung her coat on the hook.

Following Misty into the kitchen, she filled up the cat dish with a mixture of tinned and dried food then emptied the litter tray. Anything to keep her busy. Every now and then she passed by her mobile sitting on the kitchen table, touching it to bring the screen back to life. Nothing, no contact whatsoever. *Is my evening going to be as frustrating as my day turned out to be?*

Another fifteen minutes of Sara tidying up her kitchen cupboards slipped by before her phone rang. She grabbed it and without looking at the caller ID replied, "Hello. I'm here."

"Glad to hear it. Where's here?" Her brother-in-law's laughter rippled down the line.

"I'm at home. Sorry, Donald, I thought you were someone else. What can I do for you?" She was determined to get him off the line quickly but didn't want to appear rude and tell him she couldn't speak right now.

"Just checking that you're okay to pop over for Sunday lunch this week. We miss not seeing you, Sara. Especially me."

"I have a pretty hectic schedule at this moment. I'd hate to disappoint you at the last minute. Would you mind if we left it another week?"

"That'll be the third weekend on the trot you've rearranged things. You know what mum is like, she'll think that's suspicious."

"I don't care," she snapped. "Sorry, I shouldn't have said that, it's been a fraught few days. You've all got to understand I don't have a normal nine-to-five job, Donald. Even tonight, I've brought a carrier bag of work home with me. It's what I do, this is my life, and people have to accept that. Sorry, but that's how things are."

"Whoa! Okay, don't bite my head off. I'll let mum know that you'll ring her when you're free. It's been a few months since any of us have seen you, though, Sara. Take that on board before you next accept an invitation and then leave us all hanging."

"I'm sorry. What more can I say, Donald? None of this is intentional, I promise you. I never know when a killer will strike and disrupt this community. Maybe you can pass that message on to your mother for me."

"I'll put it a little more subtly than that, Sara. Mentioning killers and death is hardly appropriate language for someone still grieving their son after being gunned down by a gang, is it?"

Sara expelled a large breath. *Jesus, me and my big mouth again.* "Damn! I'm tired and hungry, desperate for my dinner, and you took the brunt of my crappy mood. Pass on my apologies and tell your mother I'll be in touch soon when work calms down a bit. I'm sure she'll understand my need to want to get a murderer off the streets ASAP."

"I dare say she will. Take care of yourself, Sara. Hope to finally see you again soon, when you're not so busy tracking down the dregs of society."

He hung up, leaving her glancing down at the phone. She shrugged. "I can't worry about whether I've upset them or not. I have more important things to contend with." She put the phone on the table and boiled a kettle to make a coffee. She had every intention of avoiding food tonight, not having much of an appetite after consuming the huge sandwich at lunchtime.

She stirred her mug at the same time her mobile tinkled that a text message had arrived. She almost tripped over Misty in her haste to get to the phone. Misty meowed and ran out of the kitchen. Pitiful tears misted Sara's eyes; she hated the thought that she'd hurt her cat, even if it was an accident.

Her hand shaking, she lifted the phone and opened the text message. An image of Mark filled the screen. His hair was damp as if the people holding him captive had either doused him in water or were torturing him that much, he was sweating. Her heart seemed to drop into her stomach. *Poor Mark. Please, hang in there, sweetheart.*

Another text arrived. She opened the message and read it out loud. "Either you get Wade released or your fella dies."

She gasped. "How the hell am I supposed to get him off the hook? They can't do this to me, to us."

She frantically typed a message of her own.

Not our problem. Ticktock. You've got until Friday to sort it out or else...

SARA DROPPED her phone on the table and collapsed into the chair. She buried her head in her hands and cried solidly for the next few minutes. Misty jumped onto her lap, her accidental kicking long forgotten, her willingness to forgive paramount.

"Misty, what am I going to do? How can they do this to us? Why can't they accept their punishment and move on? Mark is innocent. If I hadn't got involved with him, he wouldn't be in this frigging mess now. Shit! I have to save him, but how? These are ruthless thugs, with weapons. How can I combat them on my own? Even if I wanted to?"

Devastated by her inability to deliver a solution, and with the impending deadline looming, she slumped across the table, her head resting on her arm, and sobbed. Eventually, her tears dried up. She gave herself a stern talking to and did the only other thing open to her —she picked up her phone and dialled a number she rarely called.

"Hello." The woman's voice was harsh, almost unforgiving for disturbing her at this hour, or was that Sara's imagination working overtime?

"DCI Price, it's Sara Ramsey."

"Sara, are you all right?" Her tone softened. "Do you want me to come over?" she asked when Sara didn't answer.

"Please, just listen without interruption, otherwise I'm going to lose my courage and hang up."

"No, don't do that. I'll zip my mouth and open my ears. You have my full attention."

Sara closed her eyes, willing the chief to shut up. "I'm in trouble. Serious trouble, and I can't see a way out of it, hence the call."

"What type of trouble? Damn, sorry, you told me not to interrupt. Go on, I'm listening."

Sara smiled, aware that she'd be reacting the same way if the boot was on the other foot. "Mark, my new fella, has been abducted, and someone is forcing me to do something I don't want to do. I'll be damned if I do and damned if I don't, but Mark's life is in imminent danger. I need guidance. I need someone, namely you, to hold my hand through this and tell me what to do. I'm incapable of making the right decision. I no longer have faith in my abilities. Please, you have to help me... You can speak now."

The chief remained silent for the next few seconds. "My God! Okay, first of all, thank you for having the courage to tell me what's going on. This is the result of that text you had, isn't it? The gang involved in your husband's death? Shit, you finished with Mark to protect him and yet here you are telling me that they've nabbed him."

Sara let out a shuddering breath. "Yes. You're right, there are no flies on you, ma'am."

"Jesus! What do they want from you, Sara?"

"You know I told you that their leader had been arrested? Well, they want me to ensure he's released. How the fuck they expect me to do that, well, I don't have a clue. I've been sat here pulling my hair out trying to think of a solution, and I've failed. The other thing I haven't told you yet is that they've given me a deadline to adhere to."

"Which is?"

"Friday, otherwise..."

"Otherwise?" Carol Price asked, softly.

"They'll kill Mark. But that's not all. They've also added another warning. Told me that if I inform my colleagues of what's going on, they'll also kill Mark."

"Hence you being stuck in an unenviable position. Jesus, well, I'm glad you saw sense and rang me. How long have they had Mark?"

"His car was outside my house when I got in from work last night. They must've been waiting for him to arrive and jumped him. I found a note sitting on the driver's seat of his car, telling me they had him. They've since sent me a few texts and a video image of Mark." She swallowed noisily as fresh tears ran down her cheeks. "They have him tied to a chair. Wait, I did receive a call from whoever is in charge with the instructions. Sorry, my mind is all over the place. Before the guy ended the call, I heard Mark cry out in pain. He's a damned vet, for fuck's sake. If they damage his hands or fingers, he can say goodbye to his career...all because he chose to get involved with me."

"Stop that! There's no point in you beating yourself up. There was no way either of you could know anything like this would happen. Life's shit at the best of times. It just so happens that at this moment your life is far shittier than most. Hang in there. We'll sort this now that you've had the courage to ask for my help. I won't let you down, Sara. However, what I'm about to say is going to go against the grain with you."

"What's that?"

"We're going to have to inform the DI in charge of your husband's case."

"No! We can't. They'll kill Mark. I won't let you jeopardise his life any more than is necessary. I just need you to pull some strings for me, that's all." Agitated, Sara ran a hand through her hair. *Why the fuck did I ring her? Dumb question. I need her.*

"Love, you're going to have to allow me to do things my way. I'll make threats if I have to. This DI Smart won't say anything, I promise, not when I threaten his career."

Sara groaned. "Please, ma'am, I'm sure you won't have to go down that route. Don't make me regret confiding in you."

"I won't. Leave things to me. I'll get on to him first thing in the morning, see if we can work something out between us. He hinted that he's come across situations like this in the past, right?"

"I suppose so. I'm just freaking out about what this damn gang is going to do to Mark. Yes, I split up with him, but that was for his benefit. Ever since I made that call ending things, I've been a lost soul."

"You don't have to say any more. I can tell how much he means to you, Sara. Have faith. We'll get him back, I promise you. Now, get some rest. You've shared your burden, let's hope that allows you to sleep tonight. You have a troubling case to deal with at the moment. I don't want you distracted. I know that's easier said than done. Leave Mark's future in my capable hands, that's an order."

"Okay, you've convinced me. Thank you, ma'am. I hope I don't live to regret plucking up the courage to make this damn call. I couldn't bear to lose someone else who has captured my heart."

"You won't. We'll see to that. I'll chat with Smart in the morning and apprise you of what he has to say soon after. Sleep well, Sara. You did the right thing telling me, I assure you."

"I hope so, ma'am. Thank you for taking me seriously. I appreciate you listening and offering to come to our aid." Sara hit the End Call button and sat back in her chair, contemplating as her hand ran the length of Misty's slender body. "I hope things turn out for the best."

Misty clawed gently at her legs, enjoying Sara's touch.

CHAPTER 9

In spite of DCI Price's assurance that she would handle Mark's dilemma, Sara had a fitful night's sleep. At one stage she dreamt of attending another funeral, dressed in black as she said farewell to Mark, all because they'd embarked on a relationship. She'd shot up in bed, sweat soaking her whole body so much that she'd been forced to take a shower and change her bedding halfway through the night.

She walked into the bathroom and studied her reflection, pulling at the slightest lines at the edge of her eyes. Could she be prematurely ageing? Probably, with the amount of shit being flung at her. Ten minutes later, applying a thick layer of makeup did very little to disguise the tiredness rimming her eyes. She doubted her capacity to have a decent night's sleep ever again, especially over the next few days. She probably wouldn't sleep through the night again without Mark by her side and out of the dangerous clutches of the gang.

Dressed in a sombre black suit that matched her mood, Sara cared for her cat's needs then drove into work. Most of the team were already at their desks by the time she arrived. She made a conscious effort to fix a smile in place when she felt it was appropriate, anything to avoid those who knew her well, such as Carla, from asking the dreaded 'what's wrong?' question.

She entered her office and began the daunting task of dealing with a larger pile of post than usual. It was that time of year, coming up to the financial year end, when everything got scrutinised by head office. They took pleasure in sending out constant reminders to those in charge hinting at where they should be reining in their budgets. What a laugh. As if she didn't work on a tight enough budget as it was. Her team should be double the size it was. Twenty years ago, that would have been the norm. Now, head office expected teams to work more 'efficiently', for want of a better word. Sara tried to ensure that happened. On the last case they'd worked, all but one team member had switched their shifts around rather than incur any overtime costs. Not every DI was capable of toeing the line like Sara, though. She wasn't sure how her male counterparts got away with the amount of overtime they billed every year, but they did. Still, her conscience was clear on that score. It was noted on her record that she remained within budget wherever necessary by thinking outside the box.

Carla knocked on the door with a welcome cup of coffee around fifteen minutes later. "Thought you might need this. Umm...we've got another body."

Sara shook her head and flung herself back in her chair. "What? There can't be?"

"Afraid so. A fisherman down by the river saw something caught on the bank opposite him. He was fishing overnight—yeah, seems impossible to me, too, but apparently night fishing is getting more and more popular in the area, according to Barry. Anyway, I digress. When daylight broke, he spotted the object, and as it got lighter, he realised that the object was a dead body."

"Where?"

"Out near Canon Bridge. The River Wye is close by."

"Word getting out is going to have a devastating effect on tourism in the area."

"You're not kidding."

Sara sipped her coffee and then shot out of her chair. "Thanks for the drink. It'll have to wait. We'd better get down there. I take it SOCO and the pathologist are already at the scene?"

"Yep, it's all in hand."

Sara tore through the incident room and shouted at the team, "Carry on where we left off yesterday, guys. Looks like we have another one. Unsure whether it's connected or not yet. Come on, Carla, we're wasting time."

Carla ran down the stairs after her. They jumped in the car and battled through the morning traffic, arriving at the scene around fifteen minutes later. Lorraine was already there, as was her team who had erected a marquee as close to the riverbank as they could manage.

"This is becoming a habit, us meeting like this," Lorraine said, a brief smile touching her lips. "Suits are in the bag over there if you'd care to tog up before I walk you through things."

Sara and Carla stepped into their suits. Sara glanced around and spotted a man sitting on the grassy bank about ten feet away. His arms were pulled around his knees, and his head was resting on top.

"I take it that's the fisherman who found the victim?"

"You'd be right in your assumption. Poor bloke was still puking when we got here. Guess it's not often he goes fishing and hooks a body."

"I thought he spotted the body close to the riverbank," Sara said.

"He did, it was a figure of speech. You really don't know me at all, do you?"

"I'm getting there. Don't get antsy with me, it's been a long night." She cringed as soon as the words left her mouth, and in her peripheral vision, she caught Carla turning her way.

"Sorry to hear that. Hey, at least you're still around to tell the tale, she's not." Lorraine gestured towards the marquee shielding the body. "Anyway, she's dressed to kill, not be killed, if you get my drift."

"As if she was on a date?" Sara suggested.

"Exactly. I examined her, she had sex before she was killed. No traces of semen, before you ask."

Sara nodded. "Well, that's different to the first victim we found. Any comparisons you can see? Or do you think we're dealing with another sicko here entirely? I fucking hope not, we've got enough on our plate already."

"Can't say my workload is any lighter than yours at present. I could do with an assistant. They're like gold dust. I wish someone would sprinkle some my way soon before I drown in dead bodies and PMs to carry out. We're not used to this shit in these parts."

"Ouch! I feel guilty about that," Sara replied.

Lorraine frowned. "What the heck is that supposed to mean? That you're a serial killer in your spare time and the spate of dead bodies showing up are down to you and your warped perversions?"

Sara's mouth dropped open in horror. She cleared her throat and shook her head vigorously. "No, that's not what I was implying at all. Just stating facts that before I arrived, the murder rates in this area were virtually non-existent."

Lorraine tilted her head and glanced at Carla. "She does have a point. Maybe we should tie her up and keep her restrained for the night, see if any other victims surface tomorrow. Judging by her theory, I don't think they will. Is it a full moon at present?" Lorraine winked at Carla who chuckled.

"All right you two, pack it in. It was merely an observation on my part."

"A pathetic one at best," Lorraine chastised.

"You've got a sharp tongue at times, Lorraine Dixon."

The pathologist grinned as if taking her words as a compliment.

"You know what, you're pathetic. Let's see this victim then." Sara barged past a sniggering Lorraine and Carla in her haste to get into the marquee.

"Stop right there, DI Ramsey," Lorraine shouted a few feet behind. "No one enters the marquee before I do."

Sara stopped dead and waited for Lorraine to whizz past her. There were days when the pathologist really ticked her off without trying too much. This was one of those days. Carla stood beside her, chuckling. She ceased when Sara glared at her.

"It would be good if we showed the victim some respect." Sara stomped ahead of her into the marquee. Her eyes were immediately drawn to the woman's long dress. "Do people wear evening gowns nowadays?"

"Doh, obviously," Lorraine replied childishly.

"Okay, that was the wrong thing to ask. Hang on, what's that around her wrist?"

Lorraine crouched beside the victim and removed the drawstring bag. The top had been sealed with tape, making it watertight. Searching in her bag beside her, Lorraine withdrew a small pair of scissors and proceeded to snip the tape. She slipped her gloved hand inside and took out some form of ID. "It's a driving licence." She held the ID up next to the victim. "Guess what?"

Sara blew out a frustrated breath. "Don't tell me, it's not her."

"And the prize for the smartest DI around goes to DI Sara Ramsey."

"Jesus, Lorraine, do you ever get tired of listening to yourself talking shit, because I know I do."

"Oops, methinks I've overstepped the mark. Sorry, pathologists behaving badly is a no-no today with you in this foul mood."

"For your information, my mood was just fine until I turned up here and you started winding me up," Sara snapped back.

"Ladies, please. We've all got the victim's best interest at heart here. The ID belongs to the Chinese girl in the bags, doesn't it?" Carla said, sounding annoyed at the constant bickering going on between Sara and Lorraine.

"Yes, nail on the head, dear girl. Nail on the head. Which means, if my powers of deduction aren't wrong, and to answer your earlier question, we are indeed dealing with the same killer, you'll be relieved to know," Lorraine said.

"Great news. Now all we need to do is find out who this victim is."

"My guess is there will be another body out there somewhere waiting to be recovered with this vic's ID attached to them."

Sara nodded. "Unless we catch the killer first. That's a possibility, too, right?"

"Maybe. Hardly likely given the rate he's killing them off, or hadn't you thought about that?" Lorraine placed the ID in one evidence bag and the tape in another then shoved them both in her medical bag.

"Wait, her address. We'll need to let her relatives know of her death. Have you forgotten the procedure, Lorraine?"

"For a split second, possibly. I do apologise. I'm eager to get her back to the lab. Needless to say, we haven't found any form of DNA close by—not such a surprise what with her floating in the river. She was more than likely dumped upstream in the hope the current would drag her down here or even farther. I'll get my team to search a few miles upstream, see what they can discover. Don't bank on them finding anything substantial, though, will you?"

"Anything they stumble across will be a bonus. Okay, we've got three bodies now; that officially makes him a serial killer. That ups the ante for me. We need to nab this bastard swiftly before he really goes on a spree." Sara chewed her lip and inhaled then exhaled a few times to steady her nerves. Her heart rate was galloping ahead of her thinking. "Anything else for us, Lorraine? If not, then we'll make a move and let you get on with things here."

"Nothing else for now. I'll be in touch should anything come to light during the PM. By the way, you never asked what the cause of death was."

Sara pointed at the woman's bruised neck. "I think that's obvious, don't you? Strangled, unless I'm way off the mark, yes?"

Lorraine applauded her. "Another gold star coming your way."

"Whatever. Ring me or email me the results of the PM ASAP, if you will. Bye for now."

CHAPTER 10

NEARLY AN HOUR AND A HALF LATER, the satnav had directed them to a small mid-terraced house in a cul-de-sac on the outskirts of Birmingham. Sara had debated passing the chore over to the local force but had decided against it, preferring to deal with the parents herself. She needed answers, the type you couldn't rely on another force that wasn't wrapped up in the case, to provide.

Sara swallowed down her anxiety as she and Carla approached the tiny house. The front garden had no lawn. It consisted of mostly grey slate and dotted here and there with plants that needed very little care to look after, such as different varieties of grasses. *Isn't that what Japanese folk call a Zen garden?* Whether it was Japanese or Chinese, it got Sara thinking about what to do with her own garden in the summer. It wasn't as if she needed a lawn for a dog; she didn't intend ever getting one of those, not with the hours she worked. It wouldn't be fair on the poor animal.

"Are you okay?" Carla asked, ringing the bell to the side of the front door.

"Sorry, miles away. A welcome distraction for what lies ahead."

Carla nodded her understanding. They listened to the safety chain being attached before the front door eased open. A tiny woman peered through the four-inch gap.

"Hello?" she asked, her accent oriental.

Sara poked her ID through the gap so the woman could study it closely. She handed it back and closed the door, removed the chain and opened it. She bowed, adding a glimmer of an uncertain smile.

"I'm DI Sara Ramsey, and this is DS Carla Jameson. Would it be possible to come in and see you for a few moments, Mrs Ming?"

The woman nodded, bared her yellow teeth and stood back behind the door. Carla and Sara stepped into the hallway and waited for her to show them into a room. The house smelt like a Chinese takeaway. It was nearing lunchtime—had they disturbed her dinner?

"Come," she motioned with her withered hand for them to join her as she walked through the house to the back room.

There they found a tiny, dated kitchen. Sara reckoned the cupboards hadn't been replaced since back in the sixties.

"You sit. I make tea."

"Mrs Ming, there's no need for you to do that. Please, take a seat. Do you speak much English?"

"English, yes, I like English. Love England. Living here, all I wanted as child."

Sara pondered going any further seeing the woman's level of English sounded restrictive. "Do you have a husband, Mrs Ming?"

"No. Husband died, many years past."

"Any other relatives living with you perhaps?" Sara knew that foreign families tended to be larger than British ones. Their cultures ensured their elderly were cared for properly in later life. She put Mrs Ming at around sixty-five, possibly older.

The woman bared her yellow teeth again and nodded. "My son. He good son. He live here, too."

"Is he here now?"

She shook her head, the smile evaporating for an instant. "No. He at work."

"Where does he work?"

"In city, for bank. He successful man. He good boy."

"Would it be possible for you to call him? We'd prefer to see you both together, if that's possible?"

She nodded frantically, her head moving up and down faster than a hammer striking a nail. "I call him. One moment." Shuffling out of the kitchen, she returned carrying a mobile phone. "I ring him now." She pressed a number and jabbered in Chinese when the phone was answered. After a while she handed Sara the phone. "You talk to him. His name Shirong. Shirong is good boy."

"Hello, Mr Ming. I'm DI Sara Ramsey of the West Mercia Police. Would it be possible for you to pop home and see us?"

"I'm at work. I can't just up and leave. What's this about?" His English sounded far better than his mother's.

"I truly wouldn't be asking if it wasn't necessary, sir. I'd rather tell you both together, if that's okay?"

"Can you come back tomorrow? I can probably arrange some time off then. It's difficult today."

"No. I'm afraid what I have to tell you can't wait." Sara was aware how news travelled fast when a body was identified. Somehow the media always found out and was sometimes guilty of revealing the identity of a victim before the relatives had been informed. Not often, granted, but it was a possibility Sara was keen to avoid nevertheless.

"Can you give me five minutes to make some arrangements? I have meetings planned, some I won't be able to postpone at such short notice."

"Do what you have to do, sir. I wouldn't be here if the matter wasn't urgent."

"I see. In that case, give me twenty minutes. Please, don't say anything to my mother in the meantime. She's very frail and has a heart problem. She's not been well lately. I'll explain more when I get there."

"You have my word on that. See you soon." The line went dead. Sara smiled at Mrs Ming and handed her the phone. "He's leaving work now and will be here shortly."

"You want tea now?"

Sara glanced at Carla who nodded. "Thank you, that would be lovely."

They watched the woman make the tea in the traditional Chinese way which she served in a tiny china teacup and saucer, no option of having milk or sugar. Mrs Ming placed the cups and saucers on the dining room table and motioned for them to sit.

They drank their drinks. Sara was surprised how much she enjoyed it, being a coffee aficionado. The atmosphere was a little strained. Mrs Ming tried to start several conversations, but her English ran out swiftly each time.

Sara was at a loss what to say to the woman apart from the obvious question. "How long have you lived in the UK, Mrs Ming?"

"Thirty-five years. My husband and me came together. He dead now."

That was a long time to live in a country and not grasp the language. Maybe some people found it more difficult than others. Sara had learnt French at school, but there was no way she could sit down and have a conversation with a French person in their native tongue.

Maybe Mrs Ming was guilty of leaving the language to her husband, her son and her daughter to master, rather than taking the time out to learn the lingo herself.

A long twenty minutes passed before Sara heard a key enter the front door. A smartly dressed Chinese man appeared at the entrance of the dining room. His brow furrowed. He marched across the room and kissed his mother on the head and then held out his hand for Sara and Carla to shake. "I'm Shirong Ming. Now, what can I do for you? Please, make it quick as I still have numerous meetings I have to attend to this afternoon. I only managed to postpone a couple."

"We appreciate you sparing us the time. Please, sir, take a seat."

His mother scurried out into the kitchen. She boiled the kettle and returned with a cup and saucer for her son. He gave her a loving smile and kissed her on the cheek. Mrs Ming retook her seat.

Sara sucked in a steadying breath. "Mr Ming, do you have a sister?"

"Yes, Chowa. Why?" He reached out to clasp his mother's hand when she repeated her daughter's name.

"When was the last time you heard from your sister?"

"Around a week ago. She was going on a course and told us not to contact her."

"What type of course?" *Hmm...the first victim said she was going on a course too. A lead at last maybe?*

"She works for a doctor's surgery here in Birmingham. I did ask her what type of course. She told me it was to do with the admin side of things. They're in the process of changing over to a new computerised system."

First a dentist and now a doctor's surgery? "I see. When is she due back?"

"On Friday. Why are you asking about my sister? Has she done something illegal?"

Sara ran a hand over her face, struggling to find the words she knew would tear the couple's world apart. "I'm sorry to have to tell you this, but your sister's body was found a few days ago."

"What? Her body?" He leapt out of his chair and paced the room.

His mother started to sob. Had she understood or was she concerned about the way her son was reacting?

"I'm afraid so. We're based in Hereford, and she was found on the edge of a forest. Where was the course she was attending?"

"Up north somewhere. Damn, I can't remember. Wait! Newcastle, I think. I thought it was strange to travel such a long distance."

"Does your mother understand what is going on? I'm concerned about her health."

He halted his pacing and returned to his seat. Gathering his frail mother in his arms, he whispered something in her ear. She gasped and immediately started crying again. He ran a hand over her greying hair and spoke to her softly. Sara presumed he was telling her that everything would be okay. Which it clearly wouldn't be, not for them going forward.

He helped his mother to her feet. "She needs to rest. I'll be back soon."

99

The couple left the room, and Sara heard them climb the stairs, and the creaky floorboards above signified that was where they had gone.

"Shit. I hated telling them."

"It's not your fault. If it's any consolation, I thought you handled it pretty well," Carla told her.

"Only pretty well? Jesus, I must be slipping." Was that because she was distracted by what was going on with Mark? She thought she'd successfully put it aside. Obviously, she'd failed in that task.

"You're being too hard on yourself as usual. Shh...he's coming back."

Shirong entered the room and immediately sank into the chair next to Sara. "How did she die? I need to know."

"Sorry, sir, I don't think you need to know the details. All I can tell you is that her death wasn't a pleasant one."

"Is any death pleasant?"

"No, it's not. Can you tell me if your sister had any friends? Anyone she was close to perhaps?"

"She was close to us. What are you getting at?"

"Someone she would have confided in?"

"Me. She always confided in me. We were very close. I can't believe she's gone. This is likely to kill my mother. When you go, I'll have to take time off work. Once it sinks in...well, it was bad enough losing my father last year. Burying him took ten years off her life. Burying her daughter is likely to take more than that. She's not well, and her heart can't stand any more heartbreak."

"I'm sorry to hear that. If there was any way around this, I would have thought of one. The last thing I wanted to do was put your mother's life in jeopardy when I shared the news. Maybe I should have insisted on telling you by yourself."

"The truth would still have come out. Parents shouldn't expect to deal with the death of a child. It rarely happens in our culture. My parents came here all those years ago to start a new life. At the time, communism was rife in China. My father was in danger every day he walked the streets. He was a solicitor. At the earliest opportunity, after my parents had gathered enough money, they hopped on a boat and headed to the UK. They came here thinking this country would be a safe place for them to bring up their family. How wrong they were. Who did this to my lovely sister? Why would they be forced to take her life? In what circumstances? I'm sorry, I have so many questions."

"I completely understand. We are dealing with several murders in the area that appear to be connected. Your sister's ID was found attached to another victim, hence the delay in telling you of her death. We had no idea who your sister was until earlier today. We drove here the second we found out to ensure you learnt about her death from us and not through the media. I don't have all the answers you're seeking. For that I'm truly sorry. But I can give you the assurance that we will get to the bottom of this and bring the person responsible to justice, not just for your sake, but for the sake of the other victims' families as well."

"I'm glad to hear that; however, it will never ease the grief I am feeling or the concern I have for my mother's health. I fear what will happen if I leave her for an instant. This news will impact both our lives in the future, not only for a few days but for the weeks and months ahead, if she survives that long." He placed his elbows on the table and covered his head with his hands.

"I'm sorry." Two words that felt inadequate to voice, but what else could Sara say to ease this man's pain? "Is there anyone else we can call for you?"

He turned to look at her. "There's no one else left. We don't mix well with people. Our family is very tight—it *was* very tight, I mean. Now, now there are only two of us left, but for how long?"

"I can't apologise enough and I don't profess to know the extent of the pain you're experiencing, sir, but what I do know is that seeking support from a counsellor will help put things back in perspective." *The trouble is, I do know the extent of the grief and pain he's suffering at this moment. I went through months of that when Philip passed. I hope to Christ that I'm not subjected to similar pain where Mark is concerned. I'm going to do my best to ensure that doesn't happen, but first, I have a twisted fucker to track down and arrest.*

"We'll cope with what life throws at us. We don't need outsiders interfering in our grief," he retorted sharply. He ran a hand through his hair, and as a single tear dripped onto his cheek, he brushed it away. "I'm sorry. I'm suffering and striking out. Please forgive me, it's not in my nature to be nasty."

Sara offered a weak smile, one she thought fitting for the situation. "Nothing to forgive. You're hurting and have the right to show how much pain you're in. I'm going to have to ask you for the address of where your sister worked, Mr Ming."

"I can give you that. The doctor's is at the top of the road."

"We'll drop by and see if they can tell us anything further. Are you sure there is nothing you can add before we leave? Did your sister's character change in the past few months? Anything along those lines?"

He nodded. "Yes, she changed. I questioned her about it, and she said that work was placing extra stress on her. Then she came home one day and told me that she was going away on a course. She seemed happier then, as if her life was on the up, and now you come here today and tell me that her life has been ended by someone else."

"That's what it looks like. Do you know how your sister travelled to Newcastle or the name of the hotel she was staying in perhaps?"

"I dropped her to Birmingham New Street station myself. She insisted I leave her outside as it was busy. She waved me off before she entered the station. I had no idea where she was staying in Newcastle; there was no need to know that as my sister had her phone with her."

"But you said you hadn't contacted her in a week, or did I mishear that?"

"No, you're right. She called to say she had arrived and that she would ring again when she was on her way back. She told me that the course she was attending sometimes took place in the morning, the afternoon and even the evening, and she assured me that it would be better if she contacted us rather than the other way around. I listened to my sister's wishes. Didn't feel any need to doubt her word. Everyone needs their own space now and again. She had cared for my mother well since our father's death. I thought she deserved her time away from the family without her needing to feel guilty."

"You're very thoughtful, Mr Ming. We all need time to ourselves at some point."

"Yes, what I didn't expect was to never see or speak to my sister again. It hasn't quite sunk in yet. I will miss her deeply. We were very close; not every brother and sister can say that. My biggest regret is letting her go, but wait, if she was supposed to be in Newcastle and not due back until Friday, why was her body found in Hereford? That's what I'm struggling to understand."

"I agree. Maybe her employers will be able to shed some light on that. If I were to hazard a guess, maybe your sister didn't go to Newcastle after all."

"What? Why? She never lied to me. I don't understand your reasoning behind that statement, but given she was found in Hereford, who am I to say if what you're saying isn't the truth? I just wish she had confided in me, there was no reason for her not to."

"As with the first victim, we have since discovered she kept secrets from her family. We don't know the ins and outs of why that is just yet, but I promise you, we will find out."

"I don't care what's happened to the other victims." He paused as if realising how callous his words sounded. "I'm sorry, I didn't mean it to come out like that. All I meant was my concern lies with my sister, not with a total stranger or strangers."

"I understood. Is there anything else you can tell us before we leave?"

"I can't think of anything. My mind is a blur. Maybe if you give me your number, I can contact you if I think of something. My time will be taken up with caring for my mother the second you leave the house, so I might not contact you for a day or two. By the way, my sister's name means 'harmony' in English."

Hot tears misted Sara's eyes. "Whenever is fine. Please, take care of your mother, and again, we're sorry for your loss."

"I'll show you out. This news has devastated us."

"I know. I want to reassure you that we won't give up searching until we've found the person who did this to your sister."

They reached the entrance. He nodded and gently closed the front door behind them.

"I feel like shit," Sara said when they jumped back in the car.

"Me, too. I'd hate to be on the receiving end of one of our visits."

Sara sighed and switched on the engine. "It's all such a mystery. Why did these girls lie to their families? We need to see what her employers say about her absence from work. My gut is telling me she wasn't on some damn computer course."

"I have to agree with you. That side of things is indeed perplexing. Unravelling it all is a necessity if we want to locate this bastard."

Arriving at the doctor's surgery at the end of the road, there were already three vehicles parked in the car park. The surgery appeared small from the outside, but when they stepped into the reception area it was as if they'd walked into Dr Who's Tardis. The building stretched way back at the rear. All the surgeries, and by the looks of the noticeboard there were at least seven of them, were on one level.

"Hello there, how can I help?" a female receptionist asked, peering over her half-lens spectacles.

Sara flashed her ID. "DI Sara Ramsey and DS Carla Jameson. Is there a practice manager we can speak to?"

"Not really. I can see if the doctor in charge can see you. May I ask what your visit is concerning?"

"About one of your colleagues, Chowa Ming."

The woman raised an inquisitive eyebrow but didn't ask any further questions. She slipped out of her chair and knocked on a door a few feet away. A stern voice beckoned her into the room. She closed the door behind her and emerged a few seconds later with a very tall man, around six-five, who had grey hair and grey furry sideburns.

"I'm the senior doctor around here. Charles Ellis. You wanted to see me about Chowa Ming?"

"Would it be possible to conduct this meeting in private, Doctor?"

"Of course. If you walk to the end of the counter, I'll let you in there."

He opened a flap in the counter, and Sara and Carla followed him into his office. He removed a chair from a stack in the corner and placed it next to the one already sitting in front of his desk.

"Please, take a seat. Now, what has Chowa done that should bring the police to her place of employment?"

"Nothing, sir. We're making general enquiries at this moment. Where is she, do you know?"

"On holiday with her family, I believe. She mentioned they were all going back to China to visit relatives for a few weeks. So I'm afraid you won't be able to speak with her for at least another week."

"Actually, we've just come from her family home, spoken to her mother and brother. They were under the impression that Chowa had been sent away on a course by the practice."

He frowned and shook his head in disbelief. "We never do that type of thing. What course?"

"Chowa told her family that you were switching over to a computerised system and that she needed the training to be able to use it."

"What utter nonsense. Our system has been computerised for years. Any training we carry out, for instance, when someone is new, we do in-house. What is the girl going on about?"

Sara chewed on her lip while he spoke. "We've yet to find out the reason behind Miss Ming telling her family one thing and you another. Sorry, Doctor, it is with regret that I have to share some bad news with you."

"Go on. What type of news?"

"Chowa Ming's body was discovered in Hereford a few days ago."

He sat forward in his chair, the colour instantly draining from his ruddy cheeks as the shock set in. Recovering, he asked quietly, "Her body, as in, she's dead?"

"That's correct."

"My God. I can't believe this. Chowa is such a nice girl. Who on this earth would kill such an inoffensive, likeable girl such as her? It doesn't make sense."

"It is a mystery, for sure. We have no idea why she and another victim have felt the need to lie to their relatives about where they were. The truth is, that's exactly what they both did."

"Both? There's another victim? So she didn't die alone, is that what you're saying?"

"No, we're dealing with two separate incidents. Actually, we have three victims, one of whom is yet to be identified."

"Oh my! That's appalling. I've never heard the like before, not in this neighbourhood. Hang on, you said her body was found in Hereford. What the hell was she doing there?"

"Again, that's what we're trying to ascertain. Would it be possible to speak to the rest of the staff? Was Chowa close to any of her colleagues? Maybe they can fill in some of the gaps for us."

"I wouldn't say she was that close to anyone in particular. Jenny on reception will be able to tell you more about that than I can." His hand slid down his face, his cheeks now lacking any colour at all. "I'm having trouble imagining what her family must be going through at this time."

"Her mother didn't take it too well. Maybe you could ring them later to check on them, possibly."

"Of course. I'll do that in a few hours. Come, let me take you back to see Jenny, unless there's anything else you want to ask me?"

"Would there be any point if you didn't know Chowa very well?"

"Sadly not. Sorry to disappoint you."

He led the way back into the reception area. Jenny was dealing with a patient. As soon as the patient left the desk and took their seat in the waiting room, Doctor Ellis requested that Jenny join them. Keeping his voice low, he said, "Jenny, maybe you can help the officers with some information about Chowa."

"Information? Such as what, Doctor Ellis?"

"I don't know. This is so hard for me to say." He glanced at Sara, looking a little distraught.

"Jenny, Chowa has passed away. She was murdered," Sara said.

The receptionist gasped and stumbled against the desk. Carla jumped forward to hold the woman upright. Dr Ellis rushed to fetch a chair and helped Carla ease Jenny into it. "What? I can't believe this. Not Chowa. You hear of this type of thing happening, but it's always to strangers. Her poor family; her mother will be devastated." She gasped a second time. "Oh Lord, this could kill her. She idolised her brother and her mother. She was always talking about them. Sorry, I'm wittering on." She shook her head and sighed.

"It's okay. It's a natural reaction. Sorry the news has come as such a shock. We wondered if you could tell us if Chowa was seeing anyone. A boyfriend perhaps?"

"Not that I know of. She kept things like that from me. Only ever mentioned what a loving family she belonged to. Seriously, this is too traumatic for words. She was such a gentle soul. You know, all her money went to her mother, to make her mother's life better."

Sara thought that was a strange declaration, considering the house they had just come from appeared to be very dated. She found it hard to believe that any money had been spent on it in recent years. Maybe the bills on the property were higher than expected. Her brother was dressed well and worked in a bank—what about his salary? Where did that go? A receptionist's salary would be far less than someone who worked in a bank, wouldn't it? The more they learnt about the victims, the muddier the water became. What the heck were they dealing with here?

"We didn't know that," Carla said, breaking into Sara's thoughts.

Sara smiled at her partner for filling in for her. "Would anyone else working here know Chowa more intimately, shall we say?"

"As in you think she might have been seeing one of the doctors?" Doctor Ellis asked, his expression one of confusion.

"Maybe. Is that possible? We need to find out what other secrets Chowa had."

Ellis cleared his throat. "I think you'll be barking up the wrong tree if you ask me. All the doctors on the staff are happily married."

"That's good to know. Would it be possible to speak to them all the same?"

"I suppose so, if that's what you want. I think you'll be wasting your time, though. Are you all right, Jenny?"

Jenny nodded and tried to stand, but her legs were still very weak, and she plonked down on the chair again.

"Stay there a moment longer," Ellis instructed. "I'll check the appointments, see if any of the doctors are available to see you now. Are you only interested in interviewing the male doctors?"

"I'd much rather see everyone. Maybe something will register with one of them. Any clues we can gather at this point will go towards helping our investigation."

"I'll see what I can do." Ellis left the reception area and knocked on several of the doors then returned to them. "Two doctors are free now. I've told them about Chowa. I hope I did the right thing. It seemed to me that it would be better to pre-warn them what to expect. Sorry if I spoke out of place."

"You haven't, Doctor. Thank you."

He showed them into the first room where a young male doctor stood behind his desk the moment they entered. After several minutes of questioning him, it was obvious he knew nothing about Chowa's personal life. They received the same negative response when they questioned all the other doctors as well.

Half an hour later, they decided they were wasting time and started back towards Hereford. On the way, Sara's mobile rang. Her heart was in her mouth with Carla in the car, just in case it was the kidnappers trying to contact her. "Hello."

"Boss, it's me, Barry. I thought you'd like to know, I've found something significant on the CCTV footage from the nightclub."

"Excellent news. We're having a crap day ourselves. What have you found, Barry?"

"The man who approached the girls in the nightclub was Asian, as in, oriental-looking, umm...not sure what the right term is, sorry."

"Interesting. Damn, we're halfway between Birmingham and the station now, too late to turn back. Even so, can you send a decent image through to my phone? Carla can ring the Ming family, see if they recognise him at all."

"Good idea. Pinging it over now, boss."

"Thanks, Barry. We should be with you within the hour. Have any of you had lunch yet?"

"Not had time, boss."

"You've got time now, right? Nip out to the baker's, grab everyone a sandwich. I'll pick up the tab when we return. I'll have a ham and tomato on brown. Carla, what do you fancy?"

"Egg mayo on white for me, Barry."

"On it now. Thanks, boss. See you soon."

He hung up and within seconds the phone tinkled that a text message had arrived. Again, Sara's heart jolted. She'd heard that sound so many damn times over the past few days. "Can you open that for me?"

Carla opened the message and studied the photo. "Seems a decent enough chap to me."

"Looks can be deceptive, as we've experienced in the past. Ring the Mings' home number, get Mr Ming's mobile number and send him the photo, see if he can recognise the man." She held her crossed fingers up in the air.

"Will do." After several minutes of contact with Mr Ming, Carla ended the call. "No good. He didn't have a clue who the man was."

"Shit. Not the outcome I was hoping to hear. Never mind. If a case needs cracking, we should realise by now, we have to do things the hard way."

Carla placed Sara's phone in her lap and said, "Oops, holy crap. What's this?"

Sara's heart raced as she glanced sideways and saw the image of Mark filling her tiny screen. "Put it away. It doesn't concern you, Carla."

"I knocked it. I wasn't being nosy, I swear. What the fuck is going on, Sara? You can't leave me up in the air like this. Is he in danger? He looks as if he is. Fuck, the people sending you the warning messages, the threats, they've got him, haven't they?"

Sara indicated and pulled over onto the hard shoulder of the motorway and put the hazard lights on. She unclipped her seat belt and swivelled in the chair to face Carla. "This can't go any further. They've warned me that if I tell anyone, they'll kill him."

Carla held a shaking hand to her face. "What? What do they want from you?"

"They instructed me to free their leader. How the effing hell I'm supposed to do that, I just don't know."

"You have to tell the chief, she has a right to know. Threats in place or not, you can't do this alone, Sara. We'll help you all we can."

"Wait, let me finish… It was eating away at me last night. I finally realised I couldn't do this alone and rang the chief. She's agreed to have a word with Smart up in Liverpool. Shit, if the gang learn that I've blabbed, they'll slit his throat. I feel like I'm living in a vortex with a frigging timebomb strapped to my damn ankle."

Carla reached out and laid her hand on top of Sara's. "I can imagine. I wouldn't want to be in your shoes, I can assure you. However, keeping this to yourself won't do you any favours. You know how it is with shits like this. They're obviously going to make threats in order to keep you compliant with their wishes. I very much doubt they'll actually go through with harming him."

Sara blew out an exasperated breath. "They already have. The person in charge rang me the other day. Before he hung up, I heard Mark scream. It curdled my blood, I can tell you. I've barely slept a wink since they took him. The only thing running through my mind is that I'm about to lose someone else I'm head over heels in love with."

"I don't get it. You finished with him. You're telling me now that you're still in love with him?"

"Yes, of course I am. I ended our relationship to keep him out of trouble. Something inside told me that I should be fearing for his life and I needed to avoid getting him involved. It didn't work. They were more than likely watching my house. I ended it with Mark during the day, and he bombarded me with messages, which I ignored. It must have played on his mind. He probably left the surgery early that evening and drove to my house. His car door was unlocked, and lying on the front seat was a note telling me they'd taken him."

"You finishing with him must have come too late. The gang were probably following the pair of you. They took the opportunity to swoop when Mark was least expecting it. Jesus, I'm so sorry for both of you. Neither of you deserve to be embroiled in this shit. They're in the wrong. They're the ones who need to be strung up by the balls. What happens now?"

"I don't know. The chief is supposed to be getting back to me sometime this afternoon. How the heck I'm keeping a clear head to run this investigation, well, I just don't know is the answer. Feel free to jump in and get me out of a hole if you think I'm drifting off. By the way, I wasn't guilty of thinking about Mark back there. I was caught up with trying to figure out what was going on with Chowa Ming."

"I'm glad you've told me about Mark. I promise not to say anything to the others. Shit, do you think they'll come after us, you and me?"

"I doubt it. It would be too risky for them to come after a couple of coppers. There again, who knows? We need to keep our wits about us at all times."

"Have they given you a deadline to meet?"

"Yes, Friday."

"Damn, that's not enough to get everything in place. I hope Mark is made of strong stuff to handle what these dickheads are possibly going to throw at him."

Sara turned back in her seat, attached her seat belt again and started the engine. "I'll let you in on a secret: so do I."

CHAPTER 11

"OKAY, I'm going to get on to the media. Let's put this fucker's face out there for all to see. He's a definite person of interest. Anyone got anything else?"

"I have," Christine called out. "While you were out, I did some digging in the database and discovered that there have been over twenty Jane Does discovered along the M5/M6 motorways in the last year or so."

Sara growled in annoyance. "What? Okay, the fact they're unidentified could be a sticking point for us as all the bodies we've discovered so far have had IDs—well, except the first one. Oh shit, what am I saying? Yes, they've had IDs, but not their own. Can we really connect them to the Jane Does?"

"Maybe he's upped his game. Wanted more of a thrill and decided to toy with us by leaving the ID of the previous victim with the more recent vic," Carla replied, scanning the whiteboard.

"You could be onto something there. One thing I know for sure. We need to track this bastard down before he adds to that staggering number. It beggars belief there are over twenty Jane Does out there. That's just sad."

The team remained silent, each lost in their own thoughts.

"Okay, let's work with what we've got and not dwell on things which have nothing to do with us. It's about time I started chasing up the PMs. I've been lax there. Keep digging, guys."

Sara marched into her office and picked up the phone. "Hi, Lorraine. Do you have time to talk?"

"You've caught me between PMs. What's up?"

"Just got back from seeing the mother and brother of Chowa Ming. They're devastated, of course, but couldn't tell us anything new. They thought she was on a course up in Newcastle; they were flabbergasted when I told them her body was found in Hereford. But the interesting part is that when we called at the doctor's surgery where she worked, they presumed she was on holiday. So we're left with a bunch of lies flying around. Lisa Taylor told a few to her friends and relatives, too."

"I feel for you. It must be tough. A bunch of lies and another unnamed victim."

"Thanks, I need all the sympathy I can get. I could also do with a few more clues to be going on with from you. Oh, wait, before you tell me that...we've also managed to find someone on CCTV footage who could be our suspect. He was seen chatting up Lisa Taylor and her friend Mandy in a nightclub. Mandy was a bit miffed the guy found Lisa attractive when she liked him."

"Ha, well, at least she's still alive to tell the tale, unlike her poor friend. Actually, I think I may have something for you."

"Oh? I'm all ears." Sara relaxed back in her chair.

"I don't know how to say this so it comes out politely, but..."

"It's not like you to be lost for words. Just say it, Lorraine."

"Well, going by past experience, I would say all three victims were prostitutes."

Sara bounced upright again and sat there with her mouth open as she contemplated the news.

"Are you still there?" Lorraine prompted.

"Jesus, yes, I'm here. There's no way. I mean, I didn't know the girls personally, but from speaking to their relatives, I just can't see it. Although..."

"Although, what?"

"It would possibly explain all the lies they told to their friends and families. Prostitutes! So this guy picks the girls up for sex and..."

"Let me stop you right there. Victim number one, Lisa Taylor, didn't have sex before she was killed."

"Well then, that's weird. I have to ask why you suspect the girls are prostitutes in that case."

"You're really going to force me to say the words?"

"Let me say it for you then: slack vaginas."

Lorraine laughed, and Sara chuckled. She knew it was wrong, but if they didn't have these bouts of light-heartedness during their working days, they'd go insane.

"You've got me on that one. Yes, you're right," Lorraine confirmed.

Sara thought about each of the victims and the attire they'd been discovered wearing. "Whoa, hang on a second. My mind is working overtime here, so bear with me. What if these girls weren't ordinary prostitutes?"

"What are you suggesting? Part-timers? That's obvious if they all had full-time jobs."

"Not exactly. Their clothes...hardly the type of clothes a run-of-the-mill prossie wears, right?"

"Ah, now I see where this is leading. You reckon they're escorts, yes?"

"Damn right I'm suggesting that. Maybe this guy is a client? He seemed well-dressed in the footage."

"Client or pimp? Maybe he was hoping to pick up new girls to add to his harem, to put the term nicely, at the nightclub."

"Hmm...you could be right. Anything else for me?"

"Nope. To most DIs that would be enough. Hang on, yes, possible traces of skin under the nails of the victim found in the river. So when you catch the bastard, that'll help."

"Oops, sorry. I didn't mean to sound ungrateful. Skin eh? That's good news. Hopefully, all the pieces of the puzzle will start slotting things together. I need to go, I have to get in touch with my contacts in the media. I've decided to try and flush the bastard out. Now we've got an image of him, that should be easy enough for us to do. If indeed the bloke in the nightclub is him. Thanks for the info, Lorraine."

"You're welcome. Go get him, tiger." Lorraine roared down the phone and laughed.

Sara ended the call, shaking her head at the pathologist's antics. She rushed back into the incident room. "Listen up, guys. Something the pathologist has flagged up needs our urgent attention." The team all turned to face her. "Looks like all three victims were prostitutes. I'll leave it up to your imagination to consider how Lorraine came to that conclusion."

"What? No way," Carla replied. "But the families, they're all so nice. Surely, they'd know if the girls had gone down that route, wouldn't they?"

"That was my first thought, so you're not alone in thinking that. Take into consideration the clothes these women were wearing at the time of their deaths—well, two of them, Lisa and the unidentified third victim."

Carla shook her head slowly. "I see which way you're leaning. Escorts, right?"

Sara applauded her partner. "Excellent. Lorraine also mentioned possible traces of skin under the third vic's fingernails which could prove valuable. I've got one more call to make. Carla, can you organise the team, start searching the internet, local papers et cetera? Let's see if we can nail this bastard. Experience tells me that time is against us. Barry, check the nightclub image against the man wearing a hat on the hotel CCTV footage." Sara strode back into her office and sat behind her desk. Lifting the phone out of its docking station, she rang the contacts she'd spoken to a few days ago and sent them the image of the man they were interested in talking to. Both the TV and newspaper contacts told her they'd do their best to run the story later that day, which was good enough for her. She finished her final call and sat back to stare out of the window at the clouds swiftly moving in the spring breeze. Her mind drifted to Mark, and she backed away quickly when tears of frustration welled up.

The phone ringing was a welcome distraction. She answered it on the second ring. "Hello. DI Ramsey."

"Sara. It's me. I don't want to discuss what I have to say over the phone. Spare me five minutes in my office, if you would." DCI Price hung up before she had the chance to answer.

"Shit!" She left her office, rushed through the door and bolted down the grey hallway to the other end. Mary smiled at her as she entered the outer office.

"Go straight through. She told me to expect you."

"Thanks, Mary." She knocked on the door and waited to be summoned.

"Come in," DCI Price bellowed.

Her heart pounding, Sara pushed open the door and entered the chief's office. "You wanted to see me?"

"I did. Get comfortable. You could be here for a while. Before I say anything, have you received any more messages?"

"No. I don't tend to get them until I'm at home and settling down for the evening. Why?"

"Inquisitive, that's all. Right, I've spent most of the morning on the phone to DI Smart in Liverpool. He's now fully aware of the situation and told me to send you his sympathies. I spoke for you and told him we can do without his sympathy, what we need is action and he's the one that needs to sign off on that. He was pretty taken aback by that—probably expected me to be out of my depth on something like this. I showed him, though. Once he realised who he was dealing with, he spoke to me as an equal, despite the rank difference, if you get my drift. Anyway, we think we've come up with a plan. Sadly, it's going to have to involve you being centre stage and in the thick of it. Are you up for that?"

Sara widened her eyes and gulped down the bile that was clogging her throat. "Can I hear what the plan is first? Do I have a choice in the matter?"

"Of course you have a *choice*. If you say no then we'll put our heads together and come up with a better solution, we'll have to."

"Okay, I'm all ears. What do I have to do?"

Once the chief had informed her of the dangerous plan which she and Smart had discussed on her behalf, the bile rushed back in her throat and threatened to emerge. DCI Price suspected what was happening and handed Sara the rubbish bin which was half-filled with screwed-up papers and a blackened banana skin. Sara emptied her stomach and pulled a tissue from the box sitting on the DCI's desk.

"Better? Look, I know this is going to be a tough ask for you. It's the only solution we could come up with at short notice. You want Mark returned unharmed, don't you?"

"Too right I do. Sorry for throwing up, that was uncalled for."

"Rubbish. The past couple of years have been an utter nightmare for you, and this dilemma you've been thrown into is bound to upset you. Do me a favour?"

"What's that, boss?"

"Have faith. In yourself, and in the team that will be watching over you when the exchange takes place." She pointed a finger at Sara. "You know what, you won't be going through this alone. Apart from the ART guys, I mean, I'll be there as well. How's that?"

"Permission to swear, boss?"

DCI Price nodded.

"That would up the frigging ante for me, to have you there watching my every step."

Carol Price tipped her head back and laughed. "When we head north together, you're going to regard me as your friend, not your boss, you hear me? I'll only be there to lend you a hand, to support you when the time comes for the exchange to take place. I won't be in charge, James Smart will be. He seems a decent chap, with his head screwed on in the right place instead of poking out of his arse like most men."

Sara chuckled in spite of the fear surging through her veins. One thought that she was struggling to push aside galloped through her mind. *Within days I could be with Philip again if the exchange goes wrong.*

"Hello, where did you go?"

"I have so many wayward thoughts filling my head at this time. I'm sorry for wandering off."

"Only one thought should be consuming you right now. That soon you'll have your fella back, safe and well."

"Hopefully. He didn't look too well in the damn video they sent me. Ahh... I have a confession to make concerning that."

Price tilted her head. "I'd like to see that video, and what confession are you talking about?"

Sara lined up the video on her phone and handed it to the chief to play. She watched Price wince before she glanced up at Sara.

"I know how bad it looks. I assure you he'll be fine."

"That's hard to believe right now. Umm...Carla knows he's been kidnapped."

"Damn, I thought we agreed to keep it under wraps." The chief tapped her pen on the desk impatiently.

"We did. I didn't do it on purpose. I gave her my phone in the car to send an image of a suspect to one of the families. When she placed the phone on her lap, she must have flicked back through my messages by mistake, and there was Mark's image on the screen. She confronted me; I had to tell her. Actually, I feel better now that she knows. Look, there are going to be times when my mind is going to wander. When that happens, she can pick up the slack when we're out and about. I trust her not to say anything to the others."

"She'd better not. If you're telling me you're not coping well with the investigation you're dealing with, maybe you should consider taking some time off. Take the rest of the week off, get this exchange with Mark out of the way, and come back fresh on Monday. Dip into your holidays if you prefer."

"No way, I'm not running out on these girls. They need me at the helm to find out the truth behind their deaths. Don't force me to take time off, boss, please."

"All right. If you promise to stay abreast of things."

"You have my word, I promise. Another piece of the puzzle slotted into place today. We have a suspect in mind—a visual of him on CCTV anyway. No name as yet. We're hoping that will come our way soon."

"Good, excellent. Let's hope you nab the bastard soon."

"That's our intention, boss. Something else came to light this morning—a couple of things really. The victims might be prostitutes, actually escorts, and we think this guy might have killed anywhere upwards of twenty other women. We have over twenty Jane Does in the system."

"Holy crap! What are you still doing sitting in my office then? Shoo...go capture this wacko. We'll chat about the travel details to Liverpool on Thursday, does that suit?"

Back to reality with a bang. "Yes, boss." Sara left her chair and walked towards the door.

"Sara. Chin up. You have my word that everything will go well."

"I wish I had your confidence. Experience tells me that these things have a habit of going wrong. I don't want to lose him, boss."

"You won't. Think positively, and everything will go according to plan."

"If you insist. I'd better get back to the investigation. Anything to take my mind off Mark's plight."

"Keep strong. Ring me if you need to chat."

"I will. Thank you, boss."

Sara left the office and returned to the incident room on heavy legs. She was tired, and the thought of working another five hours drained her.

Carla gestured for Sara to join her when she entered the room. "What do you have?"

"A few possible escort numbers to ring. Do you think it's wise ringing them, though? Won't we likely scare him off?"

"You're right. We'll do some background searches on the information before we tackle him."

"Another thought occurred to me, too. What if this bloke is the girls' pimp or whatever he chooses to call himself?"

"What's your point, Carla?"

"What would be his reason for killing them?"

"Who knows at this stage?"

"Because they've become too old? The punters prefer younger models perhaps?"

Sara scratched the side of her face as she thought. "The victims are hardly ancient, are they?"

Carla tutted. "You're right, it was a daft idea."

Sara placed a hand on her shoulder. "No idea during an investigation as difficult as this is a daft idea. Got that?"

Carla smiled. "Okay, if you say so."

"I do. I'll be in my office if you discover anything else." Sara strode into her office and glanced out of the window at the scenery she'd already grown to love in her short time living in Hereford. Her mind drifted to the night before she'd said farewell to her husband. He'd bought her a beautiful gold necklace, just because he loved her. Philip was like that, generous and eager to make her happy. That was why his death had come as such a shock to her when it had happened. Neither of them had been ready to say goodbye. She gasped for breath, a familiar pain surrounding her heart.

I need to get past this now. I have Mark to consider. He's in even more danger than Philip was. She chastised herself for regarding it as a competition between them. "Mark's predicament is even more dangerous in some ways. No, that's the wrong thing to say."

She shook her head and moved back to her desk. Work needed to be her saviour now. Her thoughts were leading her into too many dark crevices.

CHAPTER 12

HE STOOD in front of the mirror, admiring his appearance, grooming himself until he looked perfect in every way. Tonight was going to be another special occasion. One he'd enjoy immensely, no matter which way it turned out. That was wrong—he knew exactly the way it was going to end. He had the power in his fingertips to ensure the evening went the way he wanted it to go.

One final check at his Rolex, and it was time to rock and roll. He'd arranged to meet Cheryl at the restaurant he liked to take her to now and again. She was one of life's chucklers, eager to please him every time they met up. She'd be the same this evening, he just knew it. He was going to have to rein in his true feelings for her; she was a beautiful girl, but her childish demeanour irritated him.

After tonight, it would no longer matter. He picked up his keys and headed out of the door. He had a good hour's drive ahead of him. He put on some sultry music and drummed his fingers to the beat on the steering wheel during the journey up the M5 motorway. He always ensured he arrived in plenty of time. Entering the restaurant, he made himself comfortable on one of the stools at the bar and awaited her arrival. He scanned the restaurant, making up different scenarios about the punters. In truth, he'd always been a people watcher. They fascinated him. Their lives piqued his interest in more ways than one. He often wondered what they spoke about, imagining the types of conversations going on during the course of a meal.

He watched for the special touches happening under the table as well as on top. He was so deep in thought he neglected to see his guest arrive. She blew in his ear. He shuddered with sheer lust and expectation as he smiled and kissed her on the cheek.

"I was miles away. So sorry, Cheryl. My, don't you look the part? Stunning. That shade of blue suits you, my dear."

"Thank you. It was such a beautiful gift to receive. You shouldn't have, you spoil me."

He ran a hand down her blushing cheek and invited her to sit next to him. "You're worth spoiling. I sense this evening is going to be very special indeed. Champagne?"

"I shouldn't, the bubbles tickle my nose and make me giggly."

He motioned for the waiter to deliver the champagne he'd ordered prior to her arrival.

"I love your giggly nature. That's what drew me to you in the first place if you remember?"

"I do. How could I forget the night you swept me off my feet and..." She leant forward and whispered the final words against his ear, "Into your bed."

"I remember as if it were yesterday. It was a magical moment for sure. How are you?"

"I'm well. Excited about the evening ahead of us. It's been a little while since we've spent some quality time together."

"Ah, blame my workload for that. Busy, busy, always busy. I had to shift things around to be here this evening, but I know it'll be worth the hassle in the end. We should make our way to the table now. Are you hungry?"

"Ravenous, and not just for the food." She giggled.

He helped her down off the stool, ever the gentleman in her presence, and led her through the restaurant to the table the waiter had pointed out to him earlier, upon his arrival.

They spent the next few hours flirting and making gooey eyes at each other. She chose the lobster, and he went for the sirloin steak. Money was no object, not tonight. She would be worth the extra expense he was about to lavish on her. They completed their meal with a chocolate fondant that was cooked to perfection.

She wiped her mouth on her napkin and exhaled a satisfied sigh. "I'm stuffed. It was lush, though. Thank you so much for coming all this way to see me this evening. You certainly know how to make a woman feel special."

He picked up her hand and kissed the back of it. The feel of her skin against his lips sent his senses spiralling out of control. "You're worth spoiling, believe me. Where do you want to go now? Dancing?" he asked, hoping she would decline the offer and suggest something far more intimate.

"If that's what you'd like. Me, I'd prefer to spend some time alone with you. Away from the glances of those around us."

Her cheeks flared up with colour once more, and he smiled.

"Okay, finish your champagne, and we'll get out of here, while the night is still young."

They left the restaurant at just gone ten. He offered her his arm. She slipped her hand through the gap, and together they walked to his car.

"I have just the spot in mind. We can chat for a while and see where that leads."

She giggled again. "Sounds ideal to me."

He drove to a place down by the canal. He'd been here in recent weeks, searching for possible locations, with this evening in mind. He was a plotter. Always had been. Used to thinking ahead, planning to achieve what he wanted in life. And boy, did he want her.

"Fancy a walk? It's not too cold out there. I'll lend you my jacket."

"If you wouldn't mind. It's a little nippy to be dressed like this in the night air."

He walked around the front of the car. Their gazes locked through the windscreen until he reached her door and held out a hand for her to take.

They strolled along the canal, a surprising, sudden pang of guilt seeping through his veins. *She's so adorable. Can I really bring myself to do this to her? Yes, I have to. It's important for me to tie up all the loose ends. She's the final one. Then I'll be free. Richer by a few hundred thousand and free to leave this country forever.*

He slung an arm around her shoulder and guided her along the path that stretched beneath the stone arched bridge. He halted and drew her into his arms. She rested a hand against his chest and moaned gently close to his lips.

"I need you," he whispered. The words sounded breathless to his ear.

She turned and pulled him behind her, leading him back to his car. His heart raced; he was aware what lay ahead of them. It was a shame her life would end this evening. She was one of his better girls, irritating at times, but she was still an intriguing girl who had a gentle nature.

He was prepared to let her take the lead. They entered the car, and he drove a few feet away to the secluded spot, out of the glare of the streetlights which guided people in the uneven car park.

She instigated the foreplay. He let her do what she wanted and then drew her into him for a kiss. He dug in his pocket for a condom and gave it to her, instructing her to place it on him. Then he was lost. For the next ten minutes, he found himself transported to another world. A place he longed to live, free of anxieties and the constant grind of everyday life. He deserved more out of life and was about to achieve that ambition. However, first he had a job to do. With a flick of a switch, his mood changed. Instead of Cheryl doing all the work, he took over and began to dominate her. She grinned, appreciating his newly acquired leadership skills. After the deed was finished, they got dressed. He drove a few miles down the road, was about to turn left to aim closer to her home, but instead he took a right which led him onto the M5.

"My place is back that way. Where are we going?" It was a simple question which she asked in a seductive tone, no fear resonating there.

"I don't want this night to end the way it usually does. Trust me. You'll enjoy what I have in mind, I promise you."

"I do. Trust you." She snuggled down into her chair, his jacket wrapped around her.

She reached for his hand to hold. He obliged.

Several miles down the road, he pulled into the services. "What are we doing here?"

"I need to buy something. You don't mind, do you?"

She seemed sleepy, calm but very tired. "Go ahead. Wake me when you get back."

He left the car and locked her inside then entered the vast building. He returned with a can of Coke and offered her some when he opened it. She refused.

He drove another few minutes and stopped in a lay-by up the road. He finished his can of drink and turned to her. "I want more of you. Are you up for it?"

Her smile told him everything he needed to know. They kissed; he reclined her chair and climbed on top of her. She closed her eyes. His hands sought out her neck, her eyes opening when he intensified his grip.

"I'm sorry for what I'm about to do. You're a loose end."

She grappled with his hands. She tried to open her mouth to speak, but no words came out.

He snarled at her. "Accept your fate. Don't fight it. All will be over soon enough."

And it was. Her head lolled to the side, the life stripped from her body by his dangerous intent.

Returning to his seat, his gaze swept the length of the motorway, judging the distance it took for a car way off in the distance to arrive. Seconds—that wouldn't give him enough time to dump her body. He'd have to wait for the right opportunity to come his way. It was several hours before that arrived. He was aware he was taking a risk, sitting there on the hard shoulder like that. However, he was used to it; his whole life was one big risk, it had been for years.

The traffic died down enough for him to hoist her body out of the car. He laid her on the verge, wanting her to be discovered the following day. That was all part of the game, the thing that escalated the thrill of the kill to another level, the fact he knew the body was going to be found soon. It had taken him a long time to realise that—twenty deaths, in truth.

He began his journey back to Hereford, a large grin set in place.

CHAPTER 13

Sara and Carla raced to the crime scene the second they learnt about the murder. "Well, it's not like we weren't expecting another body to show up. The question is, how many more bloody bodies are going to turn up?" Sara said, crunching through the gears as she set off from the lights. She was livid—beyond livid, in fact. They needed to stop this bastard and soon, but how?

Carla sighed heavily beside her. "I could throw you a number I pluck out of the air, if that will help. Because, like you, I haven't got a frigging clue. All we have is an image of the man we suspect, no name as yet."

"I know. That's the annoying part, so near and yet so far. Just like every other investigation we work. At least we think the man is the same, the one at the nightclub and the hotel, thanks to Barry."

"Right. There's no point getting worked up about things. You know it will all slot into place when the right details come to light. That just hasn't happened yet."

"I know. Sorry for being so negative. Maybe what's going on with Mark is beginning to wear me down a little. Just ignore me."

"As you've raised the subject, any news on Mark?"

"No. I sat at home, cuddling Misty last night, staring at the phone.

Willing it to bloody ring. Nothing, no text message, no call, absolutely bugger all."

"They're messing with your head. Hang in there. Show them what a tough bitch you can be."

Sara roared with laughter. "Should I take that as a compliment?"

"Oops, yes, definitely. Don't forget, I'm here if you ever want or need to vent."

"Thanks, Carla, it means a lot. I'd rather not dwell on it and let it affect this investigation if it's all the same to you. I know to some people that would sound heartless." She placed a hand on her chest. "It doesn't mean I'm not thinking about him. Mark is in my mind and in my heart at all times."

Carla nodded. "I get where you're coming from. I would never think badly of you. You're a professional. I admire you one hundred percent for the way you're tackling this. If I were in your shoes, I would have fallen to pieces long ago."

"Thanks. I don't think we have much farther to go. Let's hope this girl is linked to the other vics and she has the third vic's ID with her."

"We live in hope."

Ten minutes later, Sara was flashing her ID at the officer standing by the crime scene tape. One lane on the motorway had been shut, allowing SOCO to erect a marquee over the victim, shielding her from the people rubbernecking in their cars as they slowed down due to the police activity.

"Knock, knock. Are you in there, Lorraine?"

A bright-red head emerged from the flaps of the tent within seconds. "I am. Get suited and booted. The van's open if you need supplies. And before you ask, yes, I believe she's connected to the other victims already sitting in my damn fridge."

"Shit! I know we were expecting, hoping even, that would be your assessment, but it still comes as a shock. We'll be back in a second."

They rushed to the pathologist's van, slipped on the necessary protective gear and returned to the marquee. Sara pulled back the flap and motioned for Carla to enter before her.

"What have we got?" Sara stared down at the pretty redhead in her beautiful turquoise-coloured evening dress and sighed. "What a waste! Sorry, go on."

"Indeed. Right, there's evidence of sexual intercourse, although I haven't detected any semen. Again, she was strangled. The bruises around her neck and the petechial haemorrhaging is a fair indicator of that."

"Any form of ID left? I was referring to the previous victim. I doubt she's going to have her own ID on her, judging by what we've found with the other victims."

"As it happens, yes. Looks to me as though this belongs to the third victim." She handed Sara a small wallet which contained a handful of credit and debit cards plus a driving licence. Sara accepted it with her gloved hand and flicked through the contents. "Carla, take this down, please."

Carla flipped open the notebook she was holding.

"Jemima Caldercott, fifteen Granger Road, Withington, Hereford. Let's hope she has a relative waiting for her at the address. If not, we'll be even farther up shit creek."

"PMA, dear. Or don't you deal with that these days?" Lorraine asked.

"Ordinarily, I'm a big advocate of it. Although I have to admit it's faded a little during this case. Okay, back to it, anything else for me?"

"Not really. Not until I conduct the PM. I'll probably be able to tell you the contents of her stomach, if that will help?"

"Why would it? If she ate out before he did the deed, that could have been in any number of restaurants. The likelihood of being around here are as remote as the location, am I right?"

"As usual. I'll let you know if anything strange shows up. Now bugger off and let me finish in here. Your lot are eager to get rid of us so they can reopen the motorway again."

"Okay, we can take a hint. Subtleness has never been a strong point of yours, has it? Get in touch once you've done the PM. We need to up the importance on this one. I'm getting pissed off with attending these scenes."

"You and me both. You only have to show up and view the body.

I'm the one who has to work her socks off at the scene and back at the lab. Maybe you're forgetting that part."

"Okay, you win in the one-upmanship stakes. See you soon, umm...not too soon, I hope."

"Yes, dear."

Sara and Carla disrobed and deposited the suits in a black sack sitting close to the tent. Sara sighed as she got behind the steering wheel and slotted her seat belt in place. "Oh well, let's hope there's someone at the address, waiting for Jemima to show up."

"If there is, it's pretty remiss of them not to lodge her as a missing person," Carla stated.

"Maybe they're used to her staying out overnight. Who knows? Don't forget the first two women told their relatives they were attending courses. Let's not cast aspersions just yet."

"You're right to chastise me. That information had slipped my mind. Sorry."

"There's no need to apologise. Sit back and enjoy the ride," Sara said, smiling at her partner who she felt was being too hard on herself.

CHAPTER 14

THEY PULLED up outside the small terraced house on what appeared to be a quiet street out in the country. There were rolling hills and fantastic views all around them.

"Not been out this way before. Lovely views," Sara observed as they walked up the path. She rang the bell.

"I've not been out here in a while. Forgot how pretty it is."

Sara heard someone's footsteps on a possibly tiled floor approaching the door on the other side. The door opened to reveal a young woman who appeared to have tumbled out of bed a few seconds before. "Yes, what do you want?"

"Hi, I'm DI Sara Ramsey, and this is DS Carla Jameson. Would it be all right if we came in to speak to you?"

"Not until you tell me what this is about."

"Jemima Caldercott, does she live here?"

"Yes, she does." The woman gasped and placed a hand over her mouth. Dropping it a second later, she asked, "Is she okay? I thought she was staying with her boyfriend for a few days."

Sara smiled at the woman. "Can we come in? We'll explain more inside."

"Sorry, yes." She threw the door open and fell back against the wall as if she was pre-empting what they were about to tell her.

"Through here?" Sara asked, pointing at the first door.

"Okay, you'll have to excuse the mess. I don't tend to tidy up until the weekend, sorry."

"It's fine. I'm the same. Not enough hours in the day, right?" Sara entered a lounge filled with second-hand furniture. A mixture of white-painted tables and a mahogany sideboard that one of the girls' relatives had palmed off on them, no doubt. The sofas had seen better days, too. They were an odd shade of blue, and the leather was severely worn and cracked in places.

The girl joined Sara and Carla and immediately flopped into one of the sofas. "Take a seat, we don't charge. Sorry, it's a habit to say that."

"No problem. I didn't catch your name?"

"Miranda Wilkes. Where's Jemima?"

"Hi, Miranda. Where did she tell you she was going?"

"She was dressed up and didn't really tell me much. I presumed she was going out with her fella. Either that or she was going to work."

"To work? Dressed up in an evening gown? What type of work?"

Miranda's gaze dropped to the floor in front of her. "She's an escort." She shuddered, her displeasure evident.

"You disapprove of her doing that?"

"Yes. Although it has nothing to do with me. We're friends; it's not like I'm her sister or anything like that. It makes me cringe the thought of men fawning all over me. Disgusting."

"Is she aware of your views on the subject?"

"Yes, fully aware. We agreed to differ on the subject. I put my foot down and made sure she never brought any of them back here. Even I have my limits. They may be high-class punters but they're what I perceive as depraved individuals if they have to pay money to get a girl to go out with them. Don't you agree?"

"Unfortunately, yes. How often did she work?"

"She's always working. Told me the more she opens her legs, the quicker her bank balance grows. Sorry if that sounded harsh. It's what she says. Don't tell me you lot have finally arrested her? I told her what she was doing amounted to prostitution, but she just laughed in my face and called me a prude. I'm not, I promise. But I'd never go out with a man for money. I have principles."

"Does she go out with them only for a night out or does it involve her usually staying out overnight with these men?"

Miranda hesitated and frowned. "I'd rather not say. I get the impression you're trying to trick me. Where is she? What has she done wrong?"

Sara issued the woman an awkward smile. "I'm sorry, it wasn't my intention to try and trick you. It's with regret I have to tell you that Jemima's body was found a few days ago. She's dead."

"No! Don't tell me that. Not Jemima! She can't be, you must have made some mistake."

"I'm sorry, there's no mistaking what I'm telling you. Are you okay? Can I get you a drink?"

Miranda nodded. "A glass of water, please. My God, I don't believe this. I tried to tell her the money wasn't worth it. It wasn't right for her to go out with these men. They've gotta be warped to expect a woman to go out with them for cash, haven't they? I stick by that thought, and now this. Jesus! Why? Why her?"

Carla left the room to fetch Miranda a drink, returning a few seconds later with a glass which she handed to her. She accepted it, spilling some of the clear liquid on her lap as her hand shook uncontrollably.

"Sorry to break the news to you like this. We're desperate to find out more. We believe we're dealing with a serial killer in the area. Jemima is the third victim we've discovered this week. Would it be possible to see her room? Maybe we can glean something in the way of clues from looking through her belongings."

"Of course. I'll do anything to help. Christ, my mind is a muddle, I can't think straight. Her room is the second door on the right at the top of the stairs."

"Thanks. Did she discuss her work in detail with you? Sorry, that came out wrong. I mean the financial aspect of things. I don't suppose she kept any paperwork? A diary or address book perhaps?" *Sara made a mental note to follow up on the search of Lisa's room at her parents' home.*

"No. I told her as long as she paid her share of the bills then I couldn't care less what she did with the rest of her money. I believe she saved a lot of it, though. By that I mean she wasn't in town every weekend having a spend up."

"I see. Okay. I'll go and take a look. Are you okay? Do you need us to ring anyone to come and sit with you?"

"No. I'll be all right. I hope you find something useful. She's quite tidy, so it should be easy to find what you're looking for."

Sara and Carla made their way upstairs and walked into Jemima's bedroom. The bed was dressed in a fuchsia pink quilt and was made. There was a bank of white wardrobes along one of the walls. Sara pulled open one of the doors and was immediately taken by how pristine the inside was. The clothes were arranged by colour on the rail, as were the shoes in the next section. In the third wardrobe there were shelves of jumpers, in varying thicknesses, depending on the season. On the bottom shelf was a pile of paperwork and a home file similar to one Sara used herself to store all her own personal paperwork. She withdrew the file and the loose paperwork and placed them on the bed.

"I'll go through this while you sift through the paperwork, Carla."

"On it. What type of thing am I searching for?"

"Possible hotel receipts. Names of punters, addresses, that's as much as I can say at present. Ultimately, we're looking for a possible link to this oriental chap."

"Okay, I'll give it a shot."

Sara knelt on the floor and opened the home file. She flipped through the tabs first. Mostly they were dedicated to household bills. It was the tabs at the back of the file that piqued her interest. "What's this? I think I have everything here that I've just asked you to try and find. Receipts for hotels."

"Okay, this might be my ignorance talking here, but why would she have receipts for hotels? Wouldn't the punters pay those? Isn't that how escorts work? Wouldn't she have just shown up at the specified location, done the deed and skedaddled out of there?"

"Perhaps. Maybe she went farther afield and had to pay for a hotel for herself, somewhere to call her base. Possible if she had a few men to see on certain nights in the same location, if that makes sense?"

"It does. I knew I was talking out of my arse," Carla said, grinning.

"Not at all. Let's get on." She plunged her hand into the back of the file. "Bingo, a little black book. Seems she was an organised person in her job as well as her home life judging by the way this room is presented."

"Hurray, maybe that will lead us to her pimp, if that's the right word for him."

"Here's hoping." Sara turned the pages one by one, slowly taking in the information. Written at the back of the book was the name Chandra Lohan. "I think I have something. Does this sound like an oriental name to you?" Sara tilted the book sideways.

"Definitely. Worth running him through the system I'd say."

Sara fished her mobile out of her jacket pocket and pressed the designated number for the station. Christine answered the call. "Hi, it's me. I need you to run a name through the database for me."

"Okay. What is it?"

Keyboard-tapping noises filled the line. "Chandra Lohan." She spelt it out for accuracy.

"Got it. Want to stay on the line or do you want me to give you a call back? Bearing in mind the system has been slightly sluggish this morning."

"Call back when you have something. Add this name to vic three on the whiteboard for me, or get one of the others to do it. Jemima Caldercott. We're at her house now, going through her paperwork. The first name I gave you struck me as a possible link to the guy we're trying to trace at the nightclub."

"Okay, leave it with me, boss."

Sara ended the call and continued her search through the file. Disappointingly, nothing else caught her attention.

She glanced up to see Miranda leaning against the doorframe, watching them. "Sorry, I couldn't help myself. I'm scared. You don't think this person might come here, you know, and harm me?"

Sara rose to her feet and walked slowly towards her. "Honestly, I don't think he will; however, it might be a good idea if you stayed somewhere else for a few days, until we've caught the person, just to be on the safe side. Can you do that?"

"I'll need to ring my friend. I'm sure she'll put me up."

"You do that. If she can't, I can arrange for a squad car to keep an eye on the house at regular intervals throughout the day and night."

"I can't be here right now, not after finding out that Jemima has been killed. I'd never sleep at night. I'll go and ring my friend. Have you found anything useful?"

Sara pointed at the notebook on the bed. "A little black book with names in it. We'll take that with us as evidence. Tell me, do you recognise the name Chandra?"

Miranda's gaze drifted off to the right. "I do. She mentioned him a few times. When she did, it always felt like the name had slipped out when it shouldn't have, if you get what I mean." She coloured up in embarrassment and changed the subject. "Why? Do you think it's him?"

"Let's just say, the man is a person on our radar."

"He's never been here, so I don't have a clue what he looks like, otherwise I'd suggest doing one of those line-ups. It would be a waste of your time and mine."

"I appreciate the thought. Ring your friend and let me know the outcome. We'll be leaving soon."

"Yes, of course." Miranda scurried along the hallway.

Sara turned back towards the bed, withdrew an evidence bag from her jacket pocket and placed the notebook inside it. "Anything else you think we should take?"

"Nothing that I can see."

"I'm going to have a final snoop in the wardrobe before we leave.

Not sure what I'm hoping to find but it can't hurt." Sara returned to the wardrobe, the section with the shelves in, and searched right near the top. Not finding anything significant there, she decided to call it a day. "Okay, let's go."

Miranda was hanging up the phone when they walked into the living room. "Any luck with your friend?"

"Yes, Susie said I can stay with her for a few days."

"That's a relief. I'm glad to hear it. We're going now. Do you want us to hang around while you pack a bag?"

"No. I think I'll be all right, but thanks anyway. Will you let me know once you've caught the bastard?"

"I will. Let me take a note of your number."

Carla handed Sara her notebook, and Miranda recited the number for her to jot down.

Then Miranda walked them to the door. "Thanks for your help, Miranda. Sorry we had to meet under such circumstances."

"Do your best, for Jemima. I know she had her faults, that's not to say she wasn't a good person. She had a heart of gold, I promise you."

"Hopefully, her notebook will be the thing that breaks the case open for us. Take care."

Sara and Carla rushed back to the car. "Why would a nice girl like Jemima become an escort?" Carla asked once they were back on the road, heading towards the station.

"I don't know. I suppose the obvious answer would be money."

Carla shook her head and pulled a face. "It abhors me to think of people selling their body for money, always has done. No matter how desperate I've been over the years, I've never considered resorting to doing that."

"My mum has a saying, 'never cast aspersions until you've walked in someone's shoes'. I think that's a good rule to live by. Too many people make judgement calls on other people's lives without knowing the full facts. Talking of which, did you see that programme about Whitney Houston a few weeks ago? Wow, what an incredible eye-opener that was. I spent most of the evening crying during the show. She was such a sad woman. A beautiful woman with a tragic soul.

From what I can tell about the victims so far, all the women seem to be polar opposite to what I'd expect an escort to be like."

"Hmm…I'm getting the same vibe as you, and no, I didn't see that programme. Might watch it on catch-up. I used to like her music, back in the day."

CHAPTER 15

THEY ARRIVED at the station around ten minutes later. Carla headed for the vending machine while Sara stopped by Christine's desk to see what she'd managed to find out. "Any luck on Lohan?"

"Yes, but not much at this point. He's a local businessman, according to his social media pages. It's definitely the man from the nightclub, if that helps."

"Wow, yes, it does. Businessman? What type of business, apart from the escort side of things?"

"I'm trying to ascertain that now, boss. All the information I've gathered so far is a tad sketchy."

"Okay, stick with it. Let me know the second you find something. Assuming it's him, I want this man sitting in a cell ASAP before he kills someone else. Don't forget we have a fourth, unnamed victim. Judging by what he's done in the past, he'll be on the lookout for another victim within the next few hours. That is unless he's already found them and they're lying dead waiting for a member of the public to stumble across their body."

"I'll let you know, boss."

Carla joined Sara in her office and placed a cup of coffee in front of her.

"Thanks, Carla. Can you help Christine? I sense we're closing in on this man. Let's ensure he doesn't slip through the net."

"I'll get on it now. Strange his name hasn't been flagged up on the system, or is it?"

"Do you think he's intentionally stayed beneath the radar in the past?"

"Makes sense to me. Perhaps he's getting a taste for killing and working up to his endgame. Who knows what goes on in the minds of these crazy fuckers?"

"Well, we mustn't forget all those Jane Does dotted along the motorways. I'll admit, he appears to have changed his MO for some reason, if he's the one who killed all those other women. There are still too many unanswered questions flying around for my liking."

"That's true. See you later." Carla left the office.

Sara opened the notebook and jotted down a few of the names she found inside. All of them were men until she came across a few at the back which she recognised—Lisa Taylor, Chowa Ming and another one she hadn't come across before, Cheryl Dyer. She rushed out of the office and called over to Carla. "Check the system for a Cheryl Dyer, will you, Carla? My gut is telling me she could be the fourth victim. Damn, I should have taken a photo of her at the scene."

Carla grinned. "I did, so we're covered there. I'll run her name now."

Sara returned to her office, her insides jangling with excitement the way they always did when she sensed she was closing in on a suspect. She had to admit, she hadn't come across one as evil as this before, neither in Hereford nor back in Liverpool. Thinking about Liverpool, she wondered how Mark was coping. She closed her eyes for a moment, imagining his smiling face and the confusion he must be dealing with, all because he'd started dating her. *Why does life have to be so damned unfair and complicated at times?*

Carla bursting into the room brought her back to reality with a thud. "You were right. I looked her up on Facebook, and yes, it's definitely her."

"Shit! I hate being right sometimes. Get an address. We need to break the news to her relatives before the day is out." Sara glanced at her watch. It was already three o'clock. Her tummy grumbled, complaining that she'd missed yet another meal in the line of duty. That would have to wait until she got home. Then she remembered she'd skipped her evening meal the night before and only managed to grab a slice of toast on the way out this morning. Her clothes were already loose on her; she couldn't afford to lose any more weight. Even so, she didn't have time to stuff her face now. They had another victim to deal with. It was just a shame she hadn't found yet more names in Jemima's notebook. What did that mean? That the killer had finally reached his last victim?

Sighing, she left the office and walked over to Barry's desk. "I found this at the third victim's house. There's a bunch of men's names in there that I need to track down. Are you up for the challenge? Can you also chase up the search at Lisa's house for me, see if uniform found anything there?" She handed him the notebook.

"You know me, boss, always up for a challenge."

"Good, I'll leave it in your capable hands. Don't contact the men. Just track down their details. We'll discuss what to do next once you've located the information. Let me know on the Lisa search ASAP though."

"No problem."

Sara wandered over to Carla's desk and peered over her shoulder. "What a shit! She was beautiful. Begs the question why she felt the need to go down the escort route. Obviously, that's yet to be confirmed, although it does seem likely at this stage."

"Heartbreaking. It has to be about the money, doesn't it?" Carla swivelled round to face her.

"Christine, have you found out what Lohan's business is yet?"

Christine leant forward and then collapsed back in her chair. "Just located it, boss. He's a loan shark of sorts."

Sara clicked her fingers. "That's the link then. My take is the women needed money for some reason, and he hooked them into working for him as escorts. Dangled a fat juicy carrot. Probably told the women all they'd have to do was go out on dates with some of his financial backers and bingo, once the girls got a taste for the money they were earning, he upped the game and insisted they could be earning far more if they were prepared to spread their legs. Pure speculation on my part, but it fits, right?"

"I think you've hit the nail with that summarisation. Damn. I'm even more determined to get the bastard now," Carla said.

"Christine, how are we doing for an address on him? DVLA give you anything?"

"Marissa was doing that for me. How's it going?"

Marissa scratched her head. "It's proving difficult."

"That can only mean one thing. If he has a car, it's probably registered to someone else. What about under the company name, Marissa?"

"I can try. What is it, Christine?"

"Lohan's Loans. Not very original."

Marissa pounded her keyboard, and within seconds she shouted, "I've got a hit. It's a Hereford address, boss. Twenty-eight Markham Road, Lugwardine."

"That's out by the river, if I'm not mistaken?" Sara asked, glancing down at Carla."

"Yep, that's right. A nice area—too nice for the likes of him."

"Nice place for someone up to no good to hide out, though. Okay, we need to split up. Carla, you and I will drive out to Lohan's address. Will, you come with us. Barry, I need you to stay here and go through the notebook for me. Maybe some of these men are Lohan's accomplices, who knows at this point? Craig, you and Scott, go and break the news to Cheryl Dyer's family. I don't have to tell you to be gentle with them, do I? Try and find out what they know about their daughter's activities. Her job, her friends. Where she was last night, that type of thing." Sara clapped. "Let's hit it, guys."

"Shouldn't someone cover his work address?" Carla piped up.

"You're right. Okay, let's switch things around. Marissa and Christine, you go to Cheryl's address, break the news to her relatives and ask the relevant questions. Craig and Scott, I need you to go to Lohan's business address. Don't go in, just walk past discreetly, see if he's there and report back to me. If he's at the location, Carla and I will shoot over and meet you there. Barry, can you organise warrants for both his home and business addresses for me, please?"

"Will do, boss. One thing before you go. The search of Lisa's room came back as a blank. I gave the officers a bollocking on your behalf for not informing us." Barry picked up the phone while the others left their seats and marched out of the incident room.

"Thanks for that snippet, Barry." Adrenaline pumped through Sara's veins. *We're so close now. I hope nothing goes wrong.*

CHAPTER 16

THEY RACED to the detached house on a secluded estate. The ideal hideout for a killer, living amongst the wealthy in the local area. The driveway was empty. "Okay, let's not get too disheartened about this. I suppose it was to be expected at this time of the day."

Sara and Carla left the vehicle and walked up the short path to the newly built home. Sara rang the bell and scanned the close. The door remained unanswered. "I'm going to take a quick look around the back. Wait here in case it opens."

There was a small alley leading up the side of the house and a gate which led to the rear garden at the bottom. Sara opened the latch on the gate. It revealed a larger than average garden for a new-build that was mostly laid to lawn. A few spindly trees and a couple of spring flowering shrubs broke up the green space. Directly in front of the patio doors was a Cotswold stone paving area with a fancy dining table and chairs adorning it. She stepped into the garden and peered through the patio door to the kitchen. Everything inside was spick and span, nothing on the countertops at all. *Are we too late? Has he cleared out?* She looked through the other set of patio doors. The lounge had the same feel about it, as if he'd moved his furniture in but there were no knickknacks anywhere on show. Was she reading more into this? Did men do knickknacks even?

She left the garden and returned to the front of the house. Carla tilted her head when she saw her. "Nothing, no sign of life around the back."

"Great! Want to start questioning the neighbours? Maybe one of them has a key."

"There'd be no point in entering the house. There's a warrant on order. Let's do things by the book on this one. You go left, and I'll take the right."

They split up and kept an eye on each other's progress after each house they knocked at. Neither of the immediate neighbours Sara managed to find at home knew anything about Chandra Lohan. He came and went like the other newcomers on the close. Nothing strange or suspect.

When Carla joined Sara at the car, she said exactly the same. No one knew anything. Why didn't people care nowadays? Were they too busy with their own lives to be concerned with what was going on under their noses? She knew one thing: when it came out in the news that they had a serial killer living on the close, she bet they'd alter their minds in the future.

In the car, Sara rang Craig and Scott. "Hi, anything at the business address?"

"We've been here a couple of minutes. Scott walked past the premises; it's closed. We thought we'd hang around for a bit, boss, just in case he's shut up shop to grab a pint of milk or something."

"Good idea. Leave it an hour and then return to base. Same here, we're leaving his house now—nothing, no sign of a car anywhere. We've questioned the neighbours, and they were as useful as a chocolate fireguard. Frustrating as it is to consider, but I think he's done a runner."

"That's a shame, boss. Okay, see you later."

Sara ended the call. She didn't bother contacting Marissa and Christine just in case they were dealing with a grief-stricken family member. She knew how uncomfortable she felt when answering the phone during such obligations.

"Damn, what a waste of time. Back to the station. We need to find this man, and quickly."

It was four-fifteen when they walked through the main entrance of the station. Sara and Carla climbed the stairs on weary legs.

Sara dug her partner in the ribs. "Hey, come on. We did our best, let's not get down about this."

"Easier said than done. How many more women is he going to kill? What if he has another address we don't know about?"

"That seems the likely option. Either that or we're too late and he's running. Something could have spooked him."

"Bound to happen, I suppose. So near..."

"Yep. Let's not dwell on it for now. We'll put our heads together and figure something out when the rest of the team get back."

Barry glanced up expectantly as they entered the incident room.

Sara pulled a face and shook her head. "Nothing. You?"

"I've gathered some information. Nothing really significant, though."

Sara perched on the spare desk next to his and rotated her aching shoulders a few times to untie the knots. "Such as?"

"A couple of the names flagged up on the system. Two of the men were arrested for kerb crawling."

"Nice. So they decided to ditch that idea and enlist the services of an escort agency instead."

"Seems that way. Want me to bring them in for questioning?"

"We'll look at doing that later. After we've caught Lohan. He has to remain our priority."

The team agreed to work late that evening, and their efforts appeared to be paying off the second Barry shouted, "Boss, we've got a hit on an ANPR. His car has been picked up on the M5 on the outskirts of Birmingham."

One thought ran through Sara's mind: she wanted to be there when the arrest was made. "Brilliant! Get the locals on it. Carla, are you up for this?"

Carla's brow creased, and she tilted her head. "Up for what?"

"We're going out there. To chase the bastard down. I want to be the one to slap the cuffs on him. I'm selfish; I don't want anyone else taking the glory. I repeat, are you up for this?"

Carla shrugged and left her chair. "I'd be an idiot to say no. Just you and me, or shall we take a couple of the men with us?"

Sara scanned the room. Craig's arm shot into the air, eager to get in on the action.

"Get your coat, Craig. Will, do you want in on this?"

"Don't mind if I do, boss."

"Barry, I need you here. Keep in contact with Carla and Will during the journey. Let them know Lohan's exact coordinates, if that's possible."

"Leave it with me, boss. It should be easy enough to track him with the number of cameras present on the streets of Brum."

"Good. Come on, gang, let's go. We've got a possible serial killer to catch."

The four of them left the incident room with the others shouting, "Good luck!" At the top of the stairs, Sara spotted DCI Price coming out of her office and heading her way.

Sara handed Carla her car keys. "You go ahead and wait in the car. I just want a quick word with the chief. I'll catch you up."

DCI Price's expression was one of concern. "Everything all right, DI Ramsey?"

"Yes, boss. At least, I hope so. We're on our way to arrest a suspect, that's the plan anyway."

"That's excellent news. Where?"

"That's the bummer. Birmingham."

"Ouch. This is the serial killer, right?"

"Yep, I'm presuming I can bill for overtime, in the circumstances."

"Of course. How are you holding up?"

"I'm trying not to think about Mark. I slip up now and again, but basically, I'm coping quite well. That will probably alter once we have this bastard sitting in a cell. Talking of which, I'd better get my skates on."

DCI Price nodded and smiled. "Go haul in your suspect. Stay safe."

Sara turned and ran down the stairs, shouting over her shoulder, "I will."

CHAPTER 17

SARA USED her siren to speed up the motorway with Craig and Will in the car behind hot on her tail. They were halfway to Birmingham when Barry told them something they really didn't want to hear.

"By the look of things, boss, I'd say he's heading for the airport."

"Shit! Okay, you know what to do. Get Christine to ring the airport, see if he's booked in on a flight, and if so, where to."

"She's on the phone now. Sitting in a damn queue."

"What? No way. Use one of the emergency numbers."

"She is," Barry replied swiftly.

"Crap. Stick with it. I'm gonna put my foot down. Wish this damn car had wings."

"Good luck. I'll let Craig know what's going on."

Sara ended the call and slammed the heel of her hand onto the steering wheel. "I'm getting a bad feeling about this."

Carla let out an exasperated breath. "Me, too. I was afraid to say it out loud. We have to grab him before…"

"I know that. Jesus, how far are we from the airport?" A motorway sign was coming up on her left-hand side. "Twenty-two miles. I suppose that's not too bad. He hasn't reached the airport yet and he'll have to check in for his flight in advance. There's hope for us yet. PMA, that's what we need, and plenty of it."

"If you say so," Carla grumbled.

The minute they arrived at the airport, they had all the information they needed to track Lohan down. He was booked on a flight to Shanghai, leaving in an hour's time.

Craig and Will joined them at the entrance.

"I think it'll be best if we stick together for now." Sara instructed. "Once we have Lohan in sight, we'll split up, just in case he does a runner. Barry has alerted the airport security, made them aware that we're on site. They'll be keeping an eye open for us, but Barry has instructed them not to get in the way. Are we ready for this? Got your Tasers to hand? If in doubt, take him down. I get the impression he'll try and grab a hostage for a shield. Be aware of that every step of the way."

Her three colleagues all nodded their understanding, and together they walked through the glass doors to the main entrance of the airport. Once inside, they immediately headed for the huge notice-board where all the flights were listed.

"There. That's the one we're after. Gate three, which is…"

"Over here." Craig pointed and rushed ahead.

"Come back here, Craig. It's important that we stay together, at least for now."

Suitably chastised, Craig returned and lowered his head.

Sara placed a finger under his chin. Their gazes met. "I love your enthusiasm. Don't ever lose that, but learn to obey orders out in the field. It could save your life."

"Sorry, boss. I'll behave."

"Right, let's go, team. Are we all clear on what the suspect looks like?" She took out her phone and showed them the picture of Lohan from the nightclub footage as a brief reminder.

They set off then. As they got closer to the booking in area, Sara slowed. The others followed her lead. Peering from behind a screen, she surveyed the crowd. There were a few Asian people in the area, waiting to board the same flight. She should have expected that. Her gaze homed in on a man standing on the other side of the waiting area. He was alone and reading a newspaper, so she struggled to see his face.

"What do you reckon? I'm not sure. I need a second opinion. Someone want to take a look for me? The guy on the far side, reading the newspaper," she told Carla who had stepped forward.

"I agree, although it's impossible to see from this angle. We need to get closer."

"Yep, you're right. Okay, then I think we should split up. Craig, you come with me, Carla you go with Will. We'll inch our way round there for a closer look. I don't have to tell you to keep it discreet, do I?"

"Nope, you don't. Come on, Will, stay close, and no heroics, got that?" Carla said as they set off.

"All right, Craig. Are you ready?" Sara asked her partner, praying he'd keep a tight rein on his enthusiasm.

"As I'll ever be. I'll keep an eye open for any other likely possibilities on the way."

"You do that. Let's stick together. Fingers crossed this is the guy we're after."

Sara kept a watchful eye on Carla and Will circling the room. Her heart rate notched up a touch with each step she took. She blew out a few deep breaths as she closed in on the man and placed her hand on the Taser in her pocket when they were within a few feet of him.

"Shit," she mumbled. "It's not him. I was frigging wrong." She glanced over at Carla and shook her head.

Carla and Will stopped dead and scanned the area. So did Sara and Craig. She peered through the crowd at the row of duty-free shops, her gaze intensifying as her need grew. Carla and Will joined her and Craig a few moments later.

"He could be in one of the shops," Carla said, reading her mind.

"Yep, but which one? If we start searching them, there's a possibility we could miss him."

"We could split up. Two remain here watching the boarding gate, and the other two search each of the shops."

"Good idea. Boys, you stay here. Carla and I will take a shufty around the shops."

"Ring us if you need backup," Craig insisted.

"Don't worry, we will. Keep vigilant at all times." She and Carla rushed across the shiny tiled floor to the shops and entered the first one.

They emerged seconds later as the shop was virtually empty. They continued their way down the concessions and returned to the marbled area outside the shops. Sara was disappointed as their search drew a blank.

"Okay, let's get back to the others." Sara's phone rang.

"We've spotted him, boss. I saw an arm poking out from behind one of the pillars and went to investigate. It's definitely him, looks like he's dyed his hair."

"Great news. We're on our way." Rushing back to where the boys were standing, Sara followed Craig's gaze over to the left and nodded. "Okay, time's marching on now. We need to make our move before it's too late. We'll grab him when he's least expecting it. He's obviously being extra cautious; innocent people don't tend to hide in public. Again, we'll split up. Stick together in our pairs, and we'll jump him if necessary. I'd rather do that than risk him pouncing on a member of the public."

The rest of the team agreed, and they split up into the same pairs they'd chosen before. They were a few feet away from Lohan when his gaze locked on to Sara's.

She smiled and mouthed. "Give it up, Lohan."

He dropped the bag he was holding and took flight. Will broke ranks with Carla and rugby tackled Lohan to the floor. The suspect's arms ended up tucked underneath his own body and that frustrated the hell out of him. He imitated a squirming snake, but Will's hefty weight pressing down on his back prevented him from getting away.

"Get off me. I've done nothing wrong," Lohan shouted. Looking at the horrified onlookers, he cried, "Help me. Police brutality."

"That's strange. We haven't even identified ourselves yet. Anyone would think you have a guilty conscience, Mr Lohan," Sara said, standing inches from his head. She had to resist the temptation to kick it.

"I haven't. I recognise filth when I see it," he spat back at her.

"Funny that. I was thinking the same when I spotted your ugly mush. Read him his rights, Will. Let's get him back to the station. He can spend the night in the cells."

"I've done nothing. I don't know what you're talking about. You've got no proof it's me you're after."

"After for what?"

"I-I don't know," he stammered.

Sara laughed. "Almost opened your mouth and dropped yourself in it then, didn't you?" She motioned for Will and Craig to slap the cuffs on.

Between them, they hoisted the suspect to his feet. He glared at Sara and Carla. Sara suppressed a shudder when she recognised the pure evil swimming in his eyes.

Craig and Will each grabbed one of his arms and steered him through the terminal to the exit. Sara picked up the bag Lohan had discarded when he'd decided to run. She let out a relieved breath. "Thank God we caught him. One less screwed-up individual walking the streets, eh?"

"Yep. He gives me the creeps. Makes me wonder what the victims saw in him," Carla said.

"Agreed. I suppose the money came into play for most of the girls, if not all of them. I'm going to ring the chief."

DCI Price must have been expecting the call; she answered it on the second ring. "DI Ramsey, tell me you've got him?"

"We have, ma'am. He'll be tucked up in a cell overnight."

"Phew...what a relief. Give yourself and your team a pat on the back from me. I'll see you in the morning. Thanks for letting me know."

"See you then, ma'am." Sara ended the call with a smile. "She was deliriously happy and told me to pass on her congratulations. I don't know about you but I'm ready for my bed."

"Are you gonna use the siren on the way back? We'd get home a lot faster."

Sara winked at her partner. "You read my mind. No excuse not to with a criminal on board."

Back at the station, Sara dismissed Carla, Craig and Will and waited around for Lohan to be booked in by the custody sergeant. Once the suspect was safely deposited in his cell for the night, Sara relaxed. She drove home on autopilot, pondering what she was going to have for dinner. She decided on beans on toast, not having much of an appetite and desperate for her bed.

She'd not been home long when a text arrived on her mobile.

FRIDAY AT FARLOW'S **Warehouse at 8p.m.**

CRAP, less than forty-eight hours away. She closed her eyes and tried to imagine the jeopardy Mark's life was in. *Hang in there, Mark. You'll soon be back home, where you belong.*

She distractedly cooked and ate her dinner, leaving half of it, then she saw to Misty's needs and went up to bed. Although her bones were tired and every limb was weary, her mind was wide awake with thoughts of what Mark was having to contend with. She tried to switch off, listening to Philip's voicemail message as a source of comfort, but it did nothing of the sort. Instead, it only highlighted the magnitude of the situation. At around three-thirty, she made herself a cup of coffee and went back to bed. The alarm woke her at seven. Her head felt foggy, almost as if someone had transplanted a pumpkin in its place overnight. One look at her reflection told her that no amount of cold water splashed on her face was going to make an ounce of difference. She shrugged and jumped in the shower.

Grabbing a piece of toast slathered in butter, she left the house and drove into work. She was the first to arrive and set about clearing the paperwork on her desk right away. Carla poked her head around the door ten minutes or so later.

"Bloody hell. I thought I looked rough this morning. You beat me hands down."

"Thanks. I forgot to do it when I came in. Can you check on Lohan for me?"

"That's not like you. Everything all right?" she asked, stepping into the office and closing the door.

"Not really. I received a text when I got home. I can't say any more than that. I'll go and see the chief when she gets in at nine."

"Shit, you can't leave me up in the air like that, Sara."

"Sorry. The less people who know the ins and outs of what is going to take place, the better."

"In other words, you don't trust me."

"Damn you, Carla. Don't do this to me. It means nothing of the sort. I have work to do."

Carla left the room and slammed the door behind her.

Sara's shoulders slumped, and she covered her head with her hands. "That's all I need, to fall out with my partner," she complained.

Putting the argument behind her, she continued to work through the post littering her in-tray. Half an hour later, she picked up the phone and dialled Carla's number. "Are you speaking to me yet?"

"Of course," came her partner's brusque response.

"Are you ready to interview Lohan?"

"Of course," Carla repeated.

"I'll be out in a couple of minutes." Sara left her desk to gaze out of the window. The scenery which usually had a calming effect on her was doing absolutely bugger all for her today. She sighed and exited the office. Passing Carla, she tapped her partner on the shoulder. "Ready?"

Carla followed Sara out of the incident room.

Sara turned to face Carla. "Can we call a truce? I hate working in an atmosphere. We need our wits about us while we interview Lohan."

"I'm okay. It's obvious you don't want to confide in me, that's fine. As long as I know where I stand."

Carla started down the stairs, and Sara grabbed her arm.

"I thought you were better than this. Why heap more stress on my shoulders? Don't you think I'm being punished enough, is that it?"

Her partner had the decency to look away, ashamed. "I'm sorry."

"I don't want you to be sorry, I just need you to understand the predicament I'm in and how much my life has been torn apart this past week. My personal life. I'm struggling to ensure the same thing doesn't happen to my career, too. You know what? I'm going to need your help to make sure that doesn't happen. Now, are you with me on this, Carla? Because if not, then I'm going to have to see about replacing you as my partner."

Eyes widening, Carla nodded. "I said I'm sorry and I meant it. Your personal life is your own affair. I'm here if you change your mind and want my help, though."

"Thank you, I appreciate that. Look, the last person I tried to protect ended up getting kidnapped and is in the process of getting tortured by the sounds of it, that's why I chose not to involve you in this. The less you know, the better, for your own safety."

"I get that. I've behaved appallingly."

Sara smiled. "On that we agree. Come on, let's go take our foul moods out on the shit who deserves it."

Carla returned a smile and nodded. "I'm up for that."

The duty sergeant nodded towards the solicitor waiting in the reception area. Sara approached the middle-aged short man and held out her hand. "Mr Sinclair, I'm DI Sara Ramsey."

"Pleased to meet you. Are you ready to proceed with the interview?"

"We are. I'll get my partner to take you to the interview room while I arrange for Mr Lohan to join us."

"Very well."

Carla motioned for the solicitor to join her, and Sara stopped at the desk to speak to Jeff. "Any problems with Lohan overnight?"

"Quiet as a church in there all night, apparently."

"Good. Maybe he's been reflecting on the crimes he's committed and he'll be amenable during the interview."

Jeff raised an eyebrow. "One can live in hope. Want me to go fetch him?"

"If you wouldn't mind. Thanks, Jeff."

She paced the area until the sergeant returned. By his side was a smug-looking Lohan.

"Ah, Inspector. I was disappointed you didn't pay me a visit in my cell last night."

Sara tutted. "And why would I do that, Mr Lohan?"

He shrugged. "Women often find me attractive and have difficulty resisting my magnetic charm."

"Jesus Christ, I've heard enough of this bullshit. Take him through, Sergeant."

Jeff rolled his eyes and yanked on Lohan's arm, steering him in the right direction. Sara regretted not having half a dozen cups of coffee since arriving. She had a feeling she was going to miss the caffeine surge. That would have helped guide her through the interview and having to stare at this vile man's face for the next couple of hours.

Walking into the room, Jeff placed Lohan in the chair next to his solicitor. They said hello to each other as if they were having a friendly meet up in a pub.

"Would anyone like a drink before we start?" Sara asked.

"Scotch on the rocks for me," the smart-mouthed Lohan ordered.

"I'll have a coffee," Sinclair said.

"Four coffees if you would, Jeff."

"Two sugars and cream in mine," Lohan said, grinning at the desk sergeant.

Jeff left the room. They waited for him to return before they started the interview. Sara could tell Lohan was going to make her life difficult over the next few hours. She reminded herself to remain calm and not to let the obnoxious shit wind her up.

Carla said the usual speech and then took a sip from her cup.

Sara cleared her throat. "Chandra Lohan, can you tell me what your relationship was with the deceased, Lisa Taylor?" She slid a photo of Lisa across the table.

Lohan folded his arms, stared straight at her, not bothering to look down, and said, "No comment." He turned to his solicitor and asked, "That's right, isn't it? I'm allowed to say that during an interview?"

"You are, and that indeed would be my advice."

"Good. Next question, Inspector?" Lohan grinned so hard his already tiny eyes shrunk even more.

Sara refused to let him get to her. Instead, she pushed Lisa's picture aside and placed a photo of Chowa Ming next to it. "What about this young lady, Chowa Ming?"

He grinned, showing off dazzling white teeth despite not cleaning them that morning. "No comment."

"Okay, and this young lady, Jemima Caldercott?"

Again, his gaze remained fixed on Sara's, and he shook his head. "No comment."

Sara threw her last dice on the table in the shape of a photo of the fourth victim. "And this lady, Cheryl Dyer?"

"No comment. Are we done now?" He picked up his cup and emptied half his drink in one go.

Sara was tempted to swipe the cup from his hand and grab him round the throat.

"Not by a long shot, we're only just beginning. You see, Mr Lohan, we have reason to believe that you were the last person to see each of these women alive, and furthermore, we also believe that you killed them."

Lohan raised a smug eyebrow, faced his solicitor and asked, "Was there a question in that statement?"

"I don't believe so."

Lohan turned back to Sara and grinned. "No comment."

The interview followed the same pathetic formula for the next hour and a half until finally Lohan roared with laughter. "Yes, okay, I killed them all. I made them into what they were, high-class whores, earning good money. Therefore, I thought I should be the one to strip them of their titles and responsibilities."

"May I ask why?"

"It was my right to do it."

"But why now?"

He scratched the side of his face. "I had no further use for them, any of them."

"Why?" Sara repeated.

"You're beginning to sound like a scratched record, Inspector. Girls like these are easily disposed of once they have outlived their usefulness."

"Talking of which, I noticed you're covered in scratches. I'm sure the victims' PMs will come back with a match for your DNA. Okay, tell me in what way they had outlived their usefulness?"

"What didn't you understand about outliving their usefulness? I no longer needed them, their services were no longer required; therefore, they were no longer useful to me," Lohan replied with a smirk.

"Why? Had you recruited more girls?"

He shook his head. "Nope."

Sara sat back in her chair, trying to exhibit that she was far more relaxed than she actually felt. "Then why? Why kill them and not just set them free? You were their pimp, right?"

A fixed grin set in place, he said, "Hardly a pimp. I was their employer."

"For your information, anyone employing girls to take money for sex in the eyes of the law is called a pimp."

"Okay, I bet a pimp doesn't earn what I'm capable of earning, though."

Sara sat upright in her chair and glared at him. "Not any more, not now you've decided to kill 'your assets'. I'm eager to hear your reasoning behind cutting your nose off. Sorry, quaint English term you might not be familiar with."

"I'm aware of it, having lived in this country for a few years. I told you, I no longer had any use for them."

"So you discarded them like rubbish, in spite of the money they harvested for you? I'm still trying to fathom out your logic there. Enlighten me, please?"

His freakish smile dropped, and he let out what sounded like an exasperated breath. "I repeat, they outlived their usefulness."

Sara pointed at him. "You see, that's the part I'm having trouble understanding. Were the girls getting too old? Because they all seemed young enough to me."

"No. Not that." The grin reappeared as if he was intent on teasing her.

"Then what was your reasoning behind such drastic action? A man with a business head such as yours just wouldn't go down that route at all...unless...I know, you were heading to China. Why? Have you had enough of the UK?"

He slow clapped her. "There is a brain in that pretty head of yours after all."

"So you had a flight booked; therefore, you needed to kill all the girls before you departed the UK?"

"Exactly. They were my property to do with as I saw fit. I no longer required their services. I treated them well before their deaths, don't worry about that."

Sara shook her head in disgust. "You call buying them dinner and having sex with them 'treating them well', is that it?"

"Not all of them. But yes, most of them had the privilege of having sex with me before they died."

Sara opened the file in front of her and read through a list of crime scenes. "Any idea what they are?"

The widening smile on his lips told her he did. "I have a rough idea, yes."

Sinclair glanced up from the notes he was making in his legal pad. Sara smiled. "For the benefit of the tape and for your solicitor's benefit, why don't you give us a clue?"

"Locations where more bodies, women's bodies, were found, if I'm not mistaken." He shrugged. "What can I say? I have a penchant for women and I like sex. Those who I thought didn't hit the mark, I killed early on. Those women who satisfied me and made me feel good about myself, well, I gave them an opportunity they couldn't refuse. If they did, I had no further use for them." He ran a hand from one side of his neck to the other.

Sara shuddered, she couldn't help it.

He tilted his head at her. "You would have been an excellent escort,

Inspector. I think you would have brought in millions, in the right setting, of course. I would have made you Queen Bee. Only offered you to the millionaire clients on my books."

"You disgust me. Interview ended at eleven-ten a.m." Sara motioned for the young male constable standing at the back of the room to take the prisoner away. "Enjoy your time in prison. I hear nonces get a special ride where you're going. Couldn't happen to a nicer chap."

"It was a pleasure, my pleasure. I'll take it on the chin whatever is thrown at me via the courts or when I'm banged up. I'll sit in my cell at night remembering how I ended their lives. That in itself will help me survive in there. Have a good day, Inspector."

After Lohan left the room, Sara cleared the desk of all the images. "That's a hell of a nasty piece of work you're representing, Mr Sinclair."

"He's a wealthy man, Inspector."

"He was!" She grinned and stood up. "Not any more."

CARLA AND SARA escorted the solicitor back to the reception area and then returned to the incident room.

They filled the rest of the team in on how the interview had gone, and Sara ordered the team to work hard over the next few days, tying up all the loose ends. They had to have everything documented ready to present to the CPS. Sara would personally ensure nothing was left out and that Lohan was punished for ending the lives of all the women he came into contact with.

After the meeting ended, Sara bobbed along the corridor to the chief's office. Mary instructed her to go straight in. Sara knocked on the door and waited for the chief's bellow.

"Ah, DI Ramsey. Come in. Take a seat and tell me all about the arrest."

Sara did as instructed and shocked the chief by recapping what the bastard had said about his victims during the interview.

"Wow, he sounds like a real lowlife."

"A bottom-of-the-tank-feeder type to me, but if you laid eyes on him in the street you'd think of him as a well-dressed man, dripping in wealth."

"Not any more, eh?"

"My sentiments exactly. Right, now that's out of the way, I can concentrate on getting Mark back. I received a text last night from our friends." She rolled her eyes, trying to make light of the situation, even though her nerves were in tatters.

"Saying what?"

"To meet at Farlow's Warehouse in Liverpool at eight p.m. on Friday."

"Okay, I'll get on to DI Smart to ensure the exchange is on track for going ahead. We're almost at the finishing line now, Sara. I know how tough it has been for you, but hang in there."

"I will. I'll have plenty of dull paperwork to keep me occupied today and tomorrow now the investigation is finished."

DCI Price laughed. "Welcome to my damn world. What time do you think we should leave tomorrow?"

"Only if you're sure you want to come along for the ride."

"Wild horses couldn't stand in the way."

"In that case, I think we should leave early. Say around four?"

"I think three, just to be on the safe side. The M5 and M6 are notoriously hectic on a Friday between five and seven."

"You're the boss, who am I to argue with you?"

"That's sorted then. Maybe we should pack an overnight bag, just in case things don't go as planned."

"Shit! Don't say that. I'm kind of banking on Smart and the ART guys making this an easy ride for us."

"I have faith in them. We'll meet in the car park at three then. I'll instruct Mary to tell people I have an emergency dentist's appointment. That should stop them from probing deeper into my absence."

"I'll come up with an excuse, not that I can think of a plausible one now, off the top of my head."

"Just make sure people don't find out what you're up to. Of course, you'd better fill Carla in as she is already aware of what's going on.

We'll go in my car. You're bound to be distracted during the journey. This way, you'll have the pressure taken off your shoulders."

"Thanks, I appreciate that." Sara closed her eyes and exhaled a deep breath. "I hope everything goes well. I'll be devastated if doing this exchange puts Mark's life in extra danger."

"Reality check needed here. His life is already in grave danger."

Sara ran a hand over her flushed cheeks. "I know. Damn. We have to nail these bastards. If we don't, there's no telling what type of stunts they'll pull on innocent people in the future."

"That's true. I have every confidence we'll take them down."

Sara left the chief's office and stopped off at the ladies' toilet on the way back to the incident room. She placed her wrists under the cold water tap to cool the heat raging within her. Then she splashed water on her cheeks. She was willing to try anything to maintain her poised exterior. The door opened, and Carla barged into the room.

"Oh, I thought you were with the chief. Is everything all right?"

"Yes, I'm glad you're here. This remains between you and me, got that?" Sara glanced sideways to check all the cubicles were empty.

"Yep, what's up?"

"The chief and I are heading north tomorrow at three o'clock. The exchange is due to take place at eight."

"You must be worried? I know I would be."

"I am. But the chief has assured me that things will go well. I have to hang on to that hope. I just want Mark back and in one piece."

Carla stepped forward and held out her arms. Sara walked into them. She struggled to hang on to the tears threatening to fall.

"It'll be fine," Carla said.

Sara pushed away from her. "Thanks for understanding."

CHAPTER 18

THE FOLLOWING TWENTY-EIGHT hours dragged by in spite of Sara maintaining her desire to remain busy both at work and at home. Once her shift had ended, she'd gone back to the house and cleaned it from top to bottom in an attempt to prevent her mind working overtime about Mark.

Now, here she was, in the passenger seat of the chief's car, just starting out on the journey that would hopefully bring Mark back to her. In what shape, she had no idea.

Sara hadn't realised how much Carol Price enjoyed the sound of her own voice until now. Stuck in the car, with no excuse to hand to escape the chief's wittering on, she resigned herself to nodding and smiling at the appropriate times during the one-sided conversation, sighing heavily when she noticed the sign for the Liverpool turn-off marked as only five miles ahead.

"Not long to go now. The satnav is telling me we're thirty minutes away from the station," the chief announced.

"The closer we get, the tighter my stomach muscles become."

"Thought you'd been quiet throughout the journey. Figured you were going through an arduous time, so I kept talking. Boy, could I do with a coffee, I'm parched."

Sara laughed. "And there was me thinking you were going for the record for non-stop chattering in a confined space."

"Ouch! I wasn't that bad, was I?"

Sara turned to look at her. Carol briefly glanced sideways at her, and Sara raised an eyebrow. "No comment. I value my job too much."

Carol took the hint and turned the stereo on. Luther Vandross filled the car. "I love him, don't you? We could choose something different if you don't like him."

"No, a bit of Luther is fine."

With only Luther's voice filling the car, the rest of the journey passed far quicker than the previous couple of hours.

Carol pulled into the visitor's car park at the police station, and together they entered the main building and flashed their IDs at the desk sergeant.

"We're here to see DI James Smart," Carol said.

"Take a seat. I'll give him a shout," the desk sergeant replied in a broad Liverpudlian accent.

Carol sat in one of the coloured plastic chairs, but Sara decided to stand. She paced the floor until James joined them.

He appeared within a few minutes. Holding out his hand, he said, "Hello, Sara, it's good to see you again. I'm just sorry it's under such dire circumstances."

Sara managed a half-smile. "Good to see you again, too, James. Is everything set? Sorry, this is my DCI and good friend, Carol Price."

"We'll leave the conversation until we're in my office. Pleased to meet you, DCI Price."

"It's Carol. I'm here in an unofficial capacity, as Sara's friend. I'll leave all the details for you two to figure out. First things first, I'm dying for a coffee."

James shook her hand and laughed. "Now that I can put right straight away. Come with me."

They walked up two flights of stairs and into a buzzing incident room that was filled with twenty or more officers.

Carol whistled. "Wow, how the other half lives, eh, Sara?"

She laughed. "I was just thinking the same. Luckily, I have a fantastic team around me, and we don't have a high crime rate to contend with, although you wouldn't think that after dealing with the last couple of major investigations that have landed on my desk."

"Imagine having a team this size around you."

"Been there, done that. I used to work here, remember. It's not all it's cracked up to be. I much prefer working with a more intimate team, such as mine." A sudden bout of guilt raced through her. She should have confided in them what was going on with Mark. *Nonsense. The less people who know, the better. They'll understand once it comes out.* She hoped so. There was a risk that keeping the truth from them could damage their relationship. Still, she had bigger fish to fry at present.

Carol nudged her when they came to a standstill outside Smart's office while he bought the coffees. "You all right? You were distracted for a moment."

"I'm fine. Regretting not trusting my own team more."

Her boss frowned. "In what respect?"

"All this. I feel guilty keeping them in the dark. I hope they forgive me when they find out."

Carol wagged her finger. "Pack that in. They'll totally understand the reasons behind you keeping things to yourself. Stop worrying about that and let's concentrate on getting your man back home safely."

"Yes, boss." She mock-saluted Carol.

James joined them and handed around the coffees. "Why don't we go into my office and we'll run through how things are going to go down this evening?"

Sara took a step back, allowing him to enter the room first. Her stomach clenched tightly as she followed him. Carol brought up the rear and closed the door behind her.

"Okay. We're going to show up at the warehouse fifteen minutes before the exchange is due to take place. That'll give us time to home in on the right location once the gang contact you with their final message. I'm presuming that's how this is going to go down. Once you receive that, I'll get in touch with the commanding officer of the

ART, who will be on standby in the vicinity awaiting their final orders."

"Sounds good to me. If I remember rightly, the warehouse is a huge area to cover. No doubt the gang will have several lookouts posted. How do you plan on combating that, James?" Sara asked, her mouth drying up through nerves. She took a sip of her hot coffee, almost scalding her mouth in the process.

"It's a risk we're going to have to take."

"I suppose there's one good thing about the location they've chosen."

James tilted his head. "What's that?"

"At least there won't be members of the general public to deal with. We have to be thankful they didn't choose somewhere like Albert Dock. Now that would have been a nightmare scenario to contend with logistically."

"Ain't that the truth. Proves one thing: the gang aren't capable of working as effectively as they have done in the past, not with the leader banged up. Our main priority is for the exchange to take place and to get Mark back, unhurt. We'll ensure you two are out of the way before the ART descend."

"Wait a minute. You said 'you two are out of the way'. You mean Sara and Mark, right?" Carol asked.

"Yes, I'm possibly pre-empting how this is going to take shape. I think the gang will ask Sara to accompany Wade in the handover."

Sara sucked in a breath. Even though something similar had passed through her own mind, hearing the words out loud sent a shiver of apprehension shooting through her. "If that's what needs to happen, then so be it. I don't really think we'll be in a position to argue with them, will we?"

"I find working on the worst-case scenario prepares you better— in instances such as this anyway. I want you to be assured that my guys will be alert at all times and on the lookout for any possible dangers."

"I should hope so," Carol piped up. She was wringing her hands in her lap.

Sara placed a reassuring hand over her boss's. "There's no need for you to be nervous. If things go wrong, there's little we can do about it."

"Excuse me? That's supposed to put my mind at ease?"

Sara shrugged and pulled her hand away. "All I'm saying is that I have faith in James, I have to. We're dealing with a notoriously vile gang. We have to accept the likelihood that things might not go according to plan. I'm resigned to that. Our hands are tied. There's no other way out of this than to do what the gang wants."

"You need your head read. I refuse to think negatively about this situation. I know it's not ideal, but we'll have trained marksmen in the area should things go awry," Carol pointed out.

James nodded. "The chief is right, Sara. Try and remain positive. If you go in there with negativity charging through you, it could lead to mistakes happening."

Sara shrugged and sipped her drink. "Consider me told then. What's next?"

"It's a waiting game until the gang contacts us. We'll leave here around seven-fifteen. We'll go in my car. Wade is already downstairs sitting in the holding cell, behaving himself the last time I heard."

"Can I see him?" The words left Sara's mouth before she'd engaged her brain.

"I'm not sure that's a good idea, Sara. You'll see him in the car. Take my word for it, the less time you get to be with this lowlife, the better. Now, I think we should grab something to eat, what say you?"

"My stomach is so full of knots, I don't think I'd be able to keep anything down."

Carol stared at her and then shook her head. "Well, I could eat a horse. I missed lunch today and I have no plans of missing out on dinner, too. How about pizza?"

"I know a fabulous pizza takeaway. Once you smell it, Sara, you'll soon change your mind. Any preference?"

"The works for me," Carol replied, rubbing her tummy.

Sara laughed. "I'm easy. I'll have what everyone else wants."

"Good. Let me place the order." He picked up the phone and

arranged for two all-day breakfast pizzas to be delivered to the station.

While they waited, they immersed themselves in slagging off the restrictive procedures head office had put in place in the last few months.

James was right about one thing—when the pizzas arrived, Sara's tummy rumbled violently. They divided the pizzas up and washed them down with a couple more coffees. It was during this time that another text arrived on Sara's phone. She read the message then passed her mobile across the desk to James.

"Okay, this is good. The exchange will take place at the rear of the property, close to the containers. I'll call Ron, the commanding officer of the ART, to bring him up to date on things."

James picked up the phone.

Sara leant over to speak to Carol. "I'm regretting eating all that pizza now. I hope it doesn't resurface anytime soon."

"You'll be fine. Remain strong."

CHAPTER 19

THE FIRST TIME she laid eyes on Wade, Sara wanted to charge at him and rip his eyes out. Two uniformed officers were leading him out to James's car.

Sara caught James by the arm. "I'm anxious about this."

"About what?"

"Okay, the gang is expecting an exchange to take place. I'm presuming they'll want only me there with Wade. They're not going to like it if I show up with you and Carol in tow, are they?"

James rubbed his chin and glanced at Carol. "She has a point. It's something I should have thought about earlier. What do you suggest?"

"That I drive your car with Wade in the back and you go with Carol. Obviously, you'll need to keep your distance. I should be safe enough, providing the ART are there as backup. It's not an ideal position to be in, but I think if we all show up in one car the gang will freak out."

"I'm not happy about this, Sara," Carol said, anger distorting her features.

Sara shrugged. "I can't say I'm exactly jumping for joy about it either, boss."

"Sara's right. This has to be the way forward. We'll be nearby."

"Ha! Nearby? With the possibility of a shootout going on, that just isn't good enough, James. Not for me," Carol stated.

Sara cleared her throat. "It's a good job you're not here in an official capacity then, Carol."

Her boss glared at her, folded her arms and stamped her foot. "Wise arse."

"That's sorted then," James said. "Here are my keys. Take care of my baby. I've heard how crap women drivers are." His eyes glinted, and a smile touched his lips.

"Ha bloody ha. I think the statistics will prove you wrong on that one, James. What you should be worried about is whether I'll be able to keep my hands off Wade—or not, once we're alone."

"I don't think I need worry about that, not when Mark is part of the exchange."

Sara winked at him. "I'll behave myself then. Are we ready?"

Carol did something that took her breath away next. She hugged her tightly and kissed her on the cheek. "May the angels be on your shoulder throughout, guiding you and Mark safely back to us, Sara."

"You daft mare. I'll be fine."

James patted Sara on the back and walked her to the car. Once she was settled and had adjusted the driver's seat, he closed the door and opened the back door to speak to Wade. "Any crap and there'll be trouble, Wade. I'm counting on you to behave yourself in the future as agreed. Don't let me regret my decision to set you free."

Sara watched the prisoner's response in the rearview mirror.

He was grinning. "You've got my word."

James shut the back door and patted the roof of the car. Sara started the engine and steered towards the exit. She watched her boss and James jump in Carol's car behind her.

"Here we go then. The beginning of the rest of my life as a free man," Wade announced, chuckling.

"For now," Sara muttered.

"What was that, bitch?"

"Nothing. I'm not going to converse with you during the journey, so give it a rest."

"We'll see. I've yet to meet a woman who could resist my charms."

Sara rolled her eyes. Wade was the second idiot to utter the same words in the past few days. The other one was safely tucked up behind bars now. Despite her warning, Wade talked non-stop all the way to the location. They pulled up beside the containers where the exchange was due to take place. She had spotted Carol's car drop back out of sight a few minutes earlier. That was when her heart rate tripled.

"I saw you, you know," Wade said.

"What? When?"

"The day your old man got in the way of those bullets."

Sara unclipped her seat belt and turned to face him, desperately trying to hang on to her temper. "What are you expecting me to say to that?"

He shrugged. "Just saying, that's all. It was a mistake."

"One that you regret making," she snapped back sarcastically.

"Yeah, of course."

"Why? Because it got you banged up?"

"Hey, bitch, you need to learn to chill when someone's trying to be nice to you."

"Really? Being nice? Or is that the guilt talking?"

"It was regretful."

"Regrettable," she amended him.

"Get you, correcting me."

"Maybe if someone had given you a decent education when you were growing up you wouldn't have ended up on the streets with a bunch of no-marks following your every move." Sara was guilty of letting him get to her. She needed to calm down before her feelings got the better of her and she ended up in hot water.

"Maybe you're right."

Sara was at a loss what to say next. She hadn't expected him to agree with her. She glanced at the clock; it was five to eight. She opened the car door to let some air in. Then, stepping outside, she went to the back of the car and pulled Wade out.

"You gonna remove the cuffs?"

"Not yet. When the others turn up."

They waited, silence laying heavy in the air until the sound of a car arriving alerted her. She swallowed down the bile that had surfaced and was lingering in her throat. She peered through the back of the car and saw Mark. His face was bruised, and his chin was resting on his chest. "By the look of things, your gang didn't hold back with their punishment. Maybe I should've stopped off to give you a pasting, too."

Wade shrugged. "I told them not to hurt him. They'd already done it, though. That's what happens when I'm not around to tell them what to do."

"He had nothing to do with this apart from going out with me. It wasn't fair to drag him into it."

"Blame them, not me. They thought they were doing me a favour. Snowy tends to jump feet first into things. What's done is done. He don't look too badly damaged to me. I've seen worse."

She shuddered and counted her lucky stars. At least Mark was alive. They'd have to be satisfied with that outcome.

"Cuffs?" He rattled the chain behind him.

"No funny business," she warned, taking the key from her pocket. She undid the cuffs and removed them from his wrists.

He ran a hand around each wrist and smiled at her. "See, that wasn't so bad. Let's do this. I wanna have a few beers with my boys."

They walked towards the other vehicle. The gang members opened all the doors and yanked Mark from the back seat. His gaze was locked on her. She smiled, but he didn't return the smile, just stared blankly at her. He'd lost weight. He was also walking with a limp. Her heart went out to him.

"Snowy, my man. Let the guy go. She's cool. We're gonna do this nice and easy, man, no grief, you got that?"

The man pushing Mark in front of him nodded, his gaze scanning his surroundings as if expecting to be pounced on.

Four feet.

Three feet.

Two feet.

"Are you okay, Mark?" Sara asked, tears welling up.

He nodded.

The exchange took place without a hitch. Sara and Mark rushed back to the car with Sara looking over her shoulder the whole time. She settled him in the back seat and told him to lie down. Then she got behind the steering wheel and pressed hard on the accelerator. The car skidded slightly. She eased off the pedal and retreated to a safe distance. Carol's car was poking out of the side of one of the turnings. She continued past it, her attention on the road. Every now and then, she glanced in her rearview mirror. The gang members were travelling behind her, maybe thirty feet or so back. She turned right at the entrance and floored it.

That was when the ART emerged. They rammed the gang's car. Gunfire started up. Sara couldn't care less what happened next. She had Mark and was determined to get them both out of there in one piece. When she glanced back at the carnage going on behind her, she spotted Carol's car following her.

She eased out a sigh of relief. "We're clear. You can sit up now, love." Tempted as she was to get out of the car and give him a hug, she stuck to the arrangements she'd made with James to return to the station.

Mark took his time sitting up, groaning as he moved.

During the journey, Sara kept a close eye on him in the mirror. He winced constantly—every time he moved, in fact. She tried to strike up a conversation with him, but his clipped responses dampened her mood. *Is he that injured? Maybe the duty doctor can be called to check him over. Perhaps I should be on my way to the hospital instead of the station.* The station appeared ahead of her. She parked Smart's car in his space and sat with the engine running until James and Carol pulled up alongside her. She switched off and asked Mark, "Are you ready for this?"

He nodded. She turned in her seat to face him, but he refused to make eye contact with her. Bugger, she was being ripped in two by his behaviour. It was as if he was blaming her for what he'd been through. Well, he had a point, it wasn't anything different to how she'd been reacting herself since his abduction. It hurt more when he was intentionally shutting her out.

James opened the back door of the car and helped Mark get out. "Do you need to see the doctor, Mark?"

He shook his head. "No. All I want to do is go home. Back to Hereford."

"All in good time, mate. We're going to need to take a statement from you first."

Sara exited the car, and Mark glared at her. "Are you hearing this? He's refusing to let me go home. Make him do that, Sara. Make it happen," he pleaded, his voice strained with emotion.

"James, is there any way we can do this another time? He's been through a rough ordeal."

Smart faced Carol for further instructions.

Carol nodded. "I think that can be arranged. Sara and her team can deal with that side of things over the next few days. Let's give him some time to get over this."

James gave a brief nod. "If that's how you want to play it. Would you mind giving me that in writing, DCI Price, to prevent my chief chewing my balls off?"

"Of course. Shall we go through? Leave these two lovebirds to it."

Sara cringed at the endearment Carol had used. She was confused by the way Mark was acting. It was as though he couldn't bear to be around her. Then it dawned on her why. He was still hurting because she had dumped him. She needed to explain why she'd been forced to do that when they were alone. Carol and James entered the station. Sara took a few steps towards Mark. He retreated the same distance.

"Mark, don't shut me out."

His gaze met hers, bore into her soul, his eyes narrowing with hatred. At least that was how it looked to her. Maybe she was feeling too sensitive and raw herself after what had happened.

"Can we go now?" Mark asked quietly.

Sara nodded and walked around Smart's car. She opened the back door to her boss's BMW and motioned for him to get in. He squeezed past her, ensuring he didn't touch her, and settled on the back seat. She attempted to join him, but he shouted, "No. Get in the front. I want to be alone."

Tears instantly welled up. She swallowed down the lump that was restricting her throat and slammed the back door shut. Glancing at the station, she saw Carol peering around the corner, spying on them. She gestured for Carol to hurry up. Within seconds, Carol had joined her, and they set off down the motorway.

Sara pulled down the visor, hoping there would be a mirror on the passenger side. There was. She kept a close eye on Mark during the journey, his face lighting up now and then as they passed beneath the intermittent streetlights along the motorway. He seemed so dejected. There was nothing either she or Carol could say to make things right. They both gave it their best shot throughout the three-hour journey. He clammed up and refused to speak.

When they finally arrived back at Hereford station, Sara hugged her boss. "Thank you for going above and beyond for us. For driving me up there and bringing us both back in one piece. I will never forget what you've done."

"Get out of here. You'll have me blubbering in a moment. Mark, it was lovely to meet you in spite of the ghastly circumstances. I'm glad you're home safely. You two get off, I'm sure you've got lots to talk about."

Sara raised her eyebrows, intimating that she doubted Mark was ever going to speak to her again. "We have. Come on, Mark, let's go home." Sara hugged the chief again and pecked her on the cheek as Mark got in Sara's car. "Wish me luck," she whispered in Carol's ear.

Carol patted her on the arm. "Give him time. None of us truly know the extent of his injuries or what he's been through."

"I wish he'd see a medical professional, but he's refused that. I'll see you on Monday."

"See how you go. Ring me if you need an extra few days off, okay?"

"Will do. Thanks again, Carol."

There was a further uncomfortable silence filling the twenty-minute journey back to Sara's house. Although Mark sat in the passenger seat, he stared out the side window the whole time. Every conversation she started remained one-sided. She was at the end of her tether by the time they got out of the car at the other end.

"Mark, please. You *have* to speak to me. Tell me what's going on in that head of yours. Don't shut me out or we'll never get past this."

"Are the keys to my car inside your house or still in the car?"

"They're in the house." Sara opened the front door and collected the bunch of keys off the small table halfway up the tiny hall.

He held out his hand, expecting her to deposit the keys in it. She didn't. She stubbornly waited until his gaze drifted up to hers, anger apparent in his eyes.

"Come inside. Let's talk about this."

"All I want to do is go home. Now, give me my damn keys."

Sara shrugged and dropped the keys in his hand. He didn't say another word, turned on his heel and unlocked his car. She was still standing on the doorstep, stunned, long after she'd watched him drive away.

"Are you all right, Sara?" Ted was walking past with Muffin.

Casting the dazed feeling aside, she smiled at her thoughtful neighbour. "I'm all right. Goodnight, Ted. Give my love to Mavis."

"I will. You take care of yourself and have a good weekend."

"You, too." Sara walked over the threshold and closed the front door behind her. She slipped down the door to the floor and wrapped her arms around her knees. Misty attempted to jump on her lap, but Sara refused to let her, choosing instead to wallow in her own self-pity. She remained in the same position for a good half an hour, trying to figure out what had gone wrong, how her life had imploded just when her heart was on the road to recovery. What had she done to deserve this? *Life sucks. Even when happiness descends, it has a way of biting you in the arse.*

EPILOGUE

Needless to say, Sara barely slept at all on Friday night. Before she flopped into bed, she rang Carla to fill her in on how the exchange had gone but neglected to tell her that Mark had driven off the second they had got home as if he couldn't face being around her. That was what had hurt Sara the most. The way he'd cast her aside as if she was a nobody, not someone who'd placed her life on the line to rescue him.

She spent most of Saturday dejected, having numerous conversations with herself, trying to figure out where it had all gone wrong between them. She left it until midday to call him. He ignored both his mobile and his house phone, which only deepened her depression.

It wasn't until six o'clock that evening that she bucked up her ideas. Told herself to move on, to stop crying over things that were out of her control. Maybe giving Mark some space, enabling him to deal with his own feelings, would resolve the issue.

Donald rang around seven. "Sara, hi. Just ringing up to see if you can still make it tomorrow. Mum's laid on a feast. She's so excited to see you. We all are."

Sara closed her eyes, imagining the effort Charlotte had gone to on her behalf. "I'll be there, Donald. But I won't be able to stay long." She owed it to Philip's family to tell them what had happened in Liverpool. After she ended the conversation with an excited Donald, she rang James Smart to find out what had gone on after the exchange had taken place.

He told her that three out of the five gang members had lost their lives, and a member of the ART was on life support in hospital after being shot in the neck.

"Damn, I'm sorry to hear that, James. What about Wade?"

"He was one of the casualties. The other two gang members are sitting in a cell, awaiting transportation to the remand centre. How's Mark, Sara?"

"I wish I knew. I guess it hit him harder than any of us anticipated. It'll probably take time for him to get over this. I'll be here when he's ready. Until that time, I'll keep my distance."

"You're a good woman, Sara. He'll be a fool if he doesn't realise how much you love him. You're a brave woman. Stay strong."

"Thanks for going along with the plan, James. If you hadn't, he wouldn't be around today."

"Hey, no problem. It's what we do, right? Enjoy the rest of your weekend, Sara."

"You, too. I've made arrangements to go and see Philip's parents tomorrow. I'll tell them what occurred, that's why I rang you."

"Tell them to ring me if they need anything clarified. They're lucky to have you on their side, Sara. Take care. Hope things work out well for you and Mark in the future. Give him time to adjust, to figure out what the hell went on."

"I will. Thanks for all your help in getting him back, James. Keep in touch."

Sara ended the call and strolled through the house into the kitchen. She opened a can of tomato soup and placed a slice of bread in the toaster. Hardly a satisfying dinner, but it was all she could face right now. While the soup was heating up in the pan, she dialled Mark's number again. The phone rang and rang, and still remained unanswered. She made a pact with herself not to give up on him, no matter how hurt she was feeling.

THE FOLLOWING DAY she made an effort to look nice for the meal with Philip's family. She wore a yellow dress as the sun was shining. It seemed to brighten her mood, if only during the journey. Charlotte and Jonathon made a huge fuss over her the second she walked through the door. Donald appeared from the kitchen, a glass of wine in his hand which he offered to Sara.

"Just half a glass for me, I'm driving. It's so nice to see you all. I apologise for not coming sooner. Life's been a little hectic workwise lately."

Charlotte hugged her. "No need for that. You're here now. You look tired, dear. Have you been sleeping okay?"

Sara sighed. "I need you all to sit down. I have something to tell you."

The three of them glanced at each other, and they all sat, clearly eager to hear what she had to say. She told them about Wade, leaving out the part about how the gang had kidnapped Mark and that an exchange had taken place. She did tell them about the vandalism the gang had carried out on her home, though.

Charlotte left her seat and rushed to sit beside her. "My God, are you all right? No wonder you appear so exhausted. You've probably been living on your nerves for months. Why didn't you tell us?"

"I couldn't, Charlotte. I had to deal with things my own way. I rang DI Smart last night, told him I was visiting today and that I'd inform you all about what went down. He said to ring him if you have any questions but wanted to pass on his assurance that the other gang members will get what's coming to them."

"You're so brave. To have this burden on your shoulders and to deal with it all by yourself. You never cease to amaze me, darling girl. Maybe Philip was watching over you. I'd like to believe he was."

"I think he was, too. I'm fine. It all worked out well in the end."

"Let me get on with dinner. You've lost far too much weight since I last saw you. Jonathon, you can give me a hand."

The couple left the lounge, and Donald sat on the couch beside her.

"What a horrendous ordeal for you, Sara. I'm so glad things turned out for the best. Not sure how I would've felt if you'd been injured." He placed a hand on her knee.

An alarm bell sounded in her head. Sara stood and crossed the room to gaze out of the bay window, overlooking the beautifully tended garden that was Charlotte's pride and joy. Thankfully, Donald remained seated.

Jonathon came to collect them both five minutes later. The table in the dining room was set out formally with the best china on show, each place setting adorned with a napkin that Sara and Philip had bought Charlotte one year for Christmas. The roast beef tasted excellent, and Sara left the table feeling stuffed. They decided to do the clearing up first before tucking into their steamed syrup sponge pudding and custard.

At around five, Sara made her excuses to leave. It was an hour's journey from Gloucester to her home. Charlotte and Jonathon hugged her, and Donald saw her out to her car.

"Maybe I can pop over during the week and take you out to dinner." he said.

"I think I'm going to be run off my feet this week. After completing an investigation, that's when the real work begins, Donald. Can we take a rain check?"

He shrugged and dipped his head towards her. She turned and offered her cheek, narrowly avoiding another awkward kiss between them. She quickly slipped behind the steering wheel and drove off before he could say anything else.

Sara dug through her CDs and popped on the love song album that was fast becoming a favourite of hers. She was a little misty eyed while she listened to some of the tracks, but it was when Celine Dion's *Think Twice* began playing that the tears she'd been holding back truly flowed. She was crying that hard when the words *look back before you close the door* filled the car, she was forced to pull over in a lay-by for a few moments to recover. If ever a song hit the nail on the head at a sadly relevant time, it was this one. She blew her nose then started on her way again, switching the radio on instead to avoid another meltdown.

She arrived home and opened the front door. Her constant companion joined her in the hallway. She cuddled Misty for the next five minutes until she'd fully recovered. A knock on the front door behind her startled her. She quickly checked her appearance in the hall mirror, wiping away some of the smudged mascara beneath her eyes before she saw who her visitor was. *It's probably Ted. Saw I was home and has come to check on me.*

A smile set in place, she pulled the door open. "Mark! What are you doing here?"

His face was stern. Her heart thumped against her ribs as she welcomed him inside her home.

He tentatively crossed the threshold and waited for her to close the door before he spoke. "Thank God you're home."

"I've been out this afternoon, visiting Philip's parents. Have you tried to ring me?"

"Yes." He grabbed her around the waist and pulled her towards him.

She was lost when his lips covered hers in a kiss that left them both breathless.

"Forgive me, Sara. I love you so much. I can't believe how foolish I've been."

"There's nothing to forgive. You went through hell, all because of me. None of this is your fault. I let you down, my love. I only dumped you to keep you out of danger."

He shook his head. "You were my saviour. You're a true heroine. You could never let me down. Can we start again?"

Tears cascaded down her cheeks. "Of course. The danger has passed now. It's time for us to get on with our lives...together."

"Nothing would make me happier. I'm a foolish man, not worthy of you. I know that now."

"You're a foolish man to think that way. I love you, Mark Fisher. This is where our life together begins."

THE END

NOTE TO THE READER

Wow, what a ride that was, I hope you agree. A challenge emotionally and professionally for Sara to overcome with the help of her team.

But wait, there's more to come from Sara and her intrepid team. In the next instalment she's up against an arsonist who sets out on a frightening agenda.

Grab your copy of Deluded here, you won't be disappointed.

Thank you for choosing to read my work, it truly means the world to me.

M A Comley

If you can find it in your heart to leave a review I'd very much appreciate it.

KEEP IN TOUCH WITH THE AUTHOR

Sign up to M A Comley's newsletter for announcements regarding new releases and special offers.
   http://smarturl.it/8jtcvv

Or follow on:
   Twitter
   https://twitter.com/Melcom1
   Blog
   http://melcomley.blogspot.com
   Facebook
   http://smarturl.it/sps7jh
   BookBub
   www.bookbub.com/authors/m-a-comley

ABOUT THE AUTHOR

M A Comley is a New York Times and USA Today bestselling author of crime fiction. To date (April 2019) she has over 90 titles published.

Her books have reached the top of the charts on all platforms in ebook format, Top 20 on Amazon, Top 5 on iTunes, number 2 on Barnes and Noble and Top 5 on KOBO. She has sold over two and a half million copies worldwide.

In her spare time, she doesn't tend to get much, she enjoys spending time walking her dog in rural Herefordshire, UK.

Her love of reading and specifically the devious minds of killers is what led her to pen her first book in the genre she adores.

Look out for more books coming in the future in the cozy mystery genre.

Facebook.com/Mel-Comley-264745836884860
Twitter.com/Melcom1
Bookbub.com/authors/m-a-comley
https://melcomley.blogspot.com

Made in the USA
Monee, IL
19 April 2022